The Chameleon's Wedding Day

The Chameleon's Wedding Day

Stories out of Lebanon

FRANCES FULLER

A LION BOOK

Copyright © 1997 Frances Fuller
The author asserts the moral right
to be identified as the author of this work

Published by
Lion Publishing plc
Sandy Lane West, Oxford, England
ISBN 0 7459 3386 6
Albatross Books Pty Ltd
PO Box 320, Sutherland, NSW 2232, Australia
ISBN 0 7324 1357 5

First edition 1997
10 9 8 7 6 5 4 3 2 1 0

Printed and bound in Great Britain by Biddles

Contents

Acknowledgments

Among the people who influenced or aided the creation of these stories, two were indispensable. My friend Maria Daoud authenticated everything Lebanese and always goaded me for another story. My son Tim read astutely, criticized severely and held up a standard higher than I could reach, although managing not to discourage me.

I also owe gratitude to Lion Publishing for asking me to write a book about Lebanon, accepting fiction in lieu of what they had in mind, and then for waiting through the years while I kept prior commitments.

Harder to measure or to shape into words is my indebtedness to all the Lebanese who shared their lives and their homes and their country with me.

The Hitchhiker

There is a certain day in every year, after a militant rain has purged the grime and obscurity of summer, when Beirut gleams white down there on its broad shelf, when from my office on the hill above I can count not only the ships in the harbor but the windows in concrete towers. On that day a sharp line is drawn along the edge of the world between the sea and the sky, emphasizing distances, stating needlessly the meaning of separations in my life.

The day had arrived, its splendor full of claws. I stood at the window, my briefcase already crammed with typed copy and dummies and undeveloped film, and saw, superimposed on the blue-white day, the disappointed face of my son.

His letter lay on my desk. "Since I don't know why I'm here, I'm dropping out before I flunk out. I don't know where I'm going either, but I'll send an address when I get there."

I left the letter lying there. The briefcase was heavy. Hurtling down the hill toward the city, squinting over the bright-green hood of my car, I plotted what I might say to the printer. I would pay for a rush job; I could come any time and correct the proof on the spot; the pictures would be ready.

Beside the road snobar trees flashed by, spears of light darting off their needles. There was a stack of apple crates, an army truck and then a woman standing, clutching a sagging sweater around her. A woman needing a ride.

I didn't think until too late. I have policies so that I don't always have to think. I jerked my little car over to the shoulder and reached to open the door.

"Can I take you somewhere?" I asked, but she had thrown herself into the seat by the time I finished the question. Her hair was fashionless and wind-blown, her makeup worn, her socks slipping down into high-heeled shoes. The vehicle rocked with the weight of her collapse.

"To the Saloomi Circle," she said, the words automatic.

What does she think I am? A taxi driver? I thought, and said aloud, "I have to turn at Hayek."

"Wherever you are going, madame," she said.

The indifference with which she said this made me look at her closely, at her peculiar disorganization, the lipstick dribbling into the corners of her mouth. I started to sense something distracted and frenzied. Her eyes wandered, bloodshot and wild. A muscle quivered under her puffy cheek. There was something else; I didn't know what. Maybe fear. Fear seeping from the pores of her skin like an odor. For a vivid moment I was afraid, too. She might do anything. And then the moment passed, and I only wondered if she were insane.

Trying to make the movement subtle, I pushed my purse farther back on the floor behind my seat, and then shoved the stick shift into a higher gear. We were passing a building whose three metal shutters each had one big hole punched through with rockets. Above it the sky was a joyous blue. Today, in this place, anything that happened would seem to fit.

So I have picked up some kind of desperate human being, I thought. Anyway, I will be civil.

"Have you been waiting long?" I asked, expecting her to start raving about the lack of transportation, the way hitchhikers often do, but she became busy with her purse. I was watching the heavy traffic developing ahead, seeing only from the corner of my eye her rough hands fumbling with the cheap metal clasp. It was a clutch purse, too small for her rather large person and too brown and shiny for her coarse black skirt.

The movement of her hands was compulsive, feverish. "My son," she said, and she was ripping a folded piece of newspaper out of the gaudy little purse. "My son, he is kidnapped." Her voice was shrill, her eyes bulging. "Kidnapped," she shouted, "kidnapped,"

thrusting the folded paper closer to my face and slapping it with torn
nails.

I needed only a glance to see that what she had in her hand was
an ad like the ones we often see in the papers, a picture of a missing
person, a few particulars, a telephone number.

"Kidnapped? How do you know?"

"Madame," she said, her tone insistent, urgent, "somebody took
him. You understand? Somebody took him. I have to find him."
When she said, "I have to find him," her right hand made a clutching
movement in the air and then struck her breast. This gesture hurt,
upset me.

"When?"

"I don't know."

"I mean, how long since you saw him?"

"Two weeks. Two weeks he didn't come." She held up two thick
fingers. "Fifteen days nobody saw him." Her bloodshot eyes grew
hotter. She thrust the picture in front of me again, a gray newsprint
impression of a young man, with a plain face and a thin mustache. I
tried to see it while watching the car in front of me as it swerved to
avoid a hole, and I was worrying about a truck coming up behind me,
threatening to pass. I hit the hole and started to feel splintered.

"Where did they get him?"

"I don't know."

"In West Beirut?" It wasn't probable that a young man would
cross the battle line, even though shooting had stopped. Still I asked.

"No, no. He doesn't go there."

"Here then? In the East?"

"I don't know. I don't know." Her voice softened and trailed off,
as though her mind were somewhere else.

"But where was he? Where do you live?" Why can't she just tell
me? I thought.

Her face was flushed, and she rolled down the window with jerks
of the handle. The air was cold. Finally she said, "Ijdeideh. He left our
house in the morning at seven o'clock. The twenty-second. He said,
I'm going to my brother's house, and I will be back for lunch."

"And he didn't come?"

"Never."

"And his brother, where does he live?"

"In Ashrafiyeh."

"Did he arrive there?" I was aware of a sympathetic panic rising in my voice, and hers was becoming raw and weary.

"No, his brother never saw him. He just disappeared."

"Between Ijdeideh and Ashrafiyeh a young man disappears? In the city streets? In the morning? It's not reasonable," I said, knowing all the time that it didn't need to be reasonable.

"It happened like that," she said.

It happened like that, I thought, to a thousand young men. We were passing a bakery and the smell of hot bread floated into the car. I groped for something hopeful to say.

"Could he have gone somewhere else?"

"Madame," she answered, turning her hands up emptily, "where could he go?"

She was right. There was no place to go. While I thought about that she was fumbling with the paper, trying to put it away again, but her hands were too uncoordinated to get it into the pathetic purse.

She will never get home, I thought. She will collapse in the street.

"A friend of ours disappeared," I told her. "The Syrian Army had him, and we got him back safe."

"It's not the Syrians," she said, sounding bitter for the first time. I wanted to ask how she knew, but she suddenly cried out, "They will kill him; they will kill him," clutching her mouth with her stubby hands.

"No," I protested, not to comfort her, but because I didn't want to hear her say it. "Don't talk like that." It was true. I knew it, the way we know suddenly something we have always known. My eyes started to burn, and the traffic to blur. I said, "Madame, what can I do to help you?"

"I don't know. I go everywhere asking everybody. I put it in the paper, and nobody calls." She jerked her thumb toward the cities on the mountain. "I have been up there now to see these two big shots, but they won't do anything."

"Was he in one of the parties?"

She glanced at me sidelong, her face suddenly intelligent, and hesitated before she said, "No."

But I looked at her directly and suggested, "The Kata'ib? Al Ahrar?"

She whispered something then, as though anyone could hear us inside a moving car, as though it could matter anyway. I thought she said, "The Kata'ib," but maybe she said something else. It was all the same. He had fought; he had made enemies.

"He is a boy," she said. "Look." The paper was folded with the picture on top.

When I looked again, I saw the face of a man.

"I will pray for him," I told her. "I don't know how to do anything else."

"Thank you," she said.

We were coming down the hill, and the buildings of Sin el Fil seemed to grow tall as we approached. It occurred to me that I would never know the end, and because I couldn't bear not knowing, I said, "How can I get in touch with you? To know what happened."

"Take the number," she said, "so you can call his brother. Do you read Arabic?" Again she shoved the paper at me.

I pulled over to the curb across from a sign that said, "Italian-made shoes." The shoes were sitting on their box lids all over the sidewalk. I read the name under the picture. Fou'ad. Lovely, poetic name. I had to reach behind the seat to retrieve my purse and then rummage in it until I found a scrap of paper, an address I thought I had lost. I wrote on the back of it. I said, "It's his brother's number?"

"Yes. Write his name. Elie Habeeb."

"Can I call just to ask if there is news?"

"Of course. Tell him you met his mother. And tell him you are praying for Fou'ad." She made it sound concrete, like organizing a search-party.

I wrote "Elie Habeeb." Then I wrote the name of his missing

brother, "Fou'ad Saadeh Habeeb." I stared at his picture. "How old is he?"

"Eighteen."

He was old for eighteen.

"I have a son who is eighteen," I told her, remembering that Rick, too, was somehow lost.

"Then you know, madame, you know." And suddenly her face cracked into pieces. Her mouth contorted, her eyes became unfocused, and a new tic jumped in her cheek.

"I will pray," I said, "as though he were my own son."

"Please," she said, "I beg you."

"I promise. I will not forget day or night."

I started to let out the clutch then and turn the wheel. Didn't I have an appointment somewhere?

"Pray they don't kill him," she said, her voice hoarse and faint. When I looked at her, she gestured with her finger across her throat and said, "They will kill him," using a word that means to slaughter an animal.

I tried not to imagine it, but the vision came too fast and irresistibly, like a nightmare. Rick's face, young for eighteen, with a knife at his throat and terror on his handsome face. Almost too weak to pull on the brake and turn off the ignition, I whispered, "No," and then "Yes."

I leaned on the steering wheel and prayed for Fou'ad, while the roar and swish of passing cars snatched away my words and beside me the woman's whispers were unintelligible and eloquent. It was so reasonable, our request, and so logical that we two should be there asking. There was no way we could be refused.

Afterwards we were quiet. She crossed herself. I saw that a vendor had arrived and parked a cartload of apples a few feet from the front of my car. When I turned toward her, her eyes became very wide, asking me some question.

"I know God heard us," I said, because it was true, but maybe it was the answer to the wrong question. She tucked the paper into her purse.

Pulling into the street again, I asked her, "What is your name?"

"Hikmet."

"I'm Jenny."

"Honored," she said, touching her chest.

"I will telephone, Hikmet. I will call Elie in Ashrafiyeh and get the news about Fou'ad. Keep hoping, because as long as he is alive, he needs you." I had such a vivid picture of how he needed someone to believe.

"Yes," she said. "We have to hope." She seemed much calmer.

At the Hayek intersection I realized that she would need to walk the few blocks to the Saloomi Circle, and I decided to take her there.

"God bless you, madame," she said. "God bless your children and keep them."

There were taxis standing; she would find a ride to Ijdeideh. I blocked one line of traffic around the circle to let her out, and somebody began honking immediately.

She thanked me again, heaping blessings on me and my children, grabbing my hand and kissing it. Half out of the car, holding the door open with the same hand in which she clutched her shiny purse, she suddenly froze, looking back over her shoulder, and her eyes were great and wild, that hint of insanity on her face again.

"Is he dead?" she said.

The question caught me unprepared so that I stammered, heard horns blowing and felt her waiting for an answer before I said, "No, never. It's not possible." I said it with intended conviction and authority, because I wanted her to get home and not go stark crazy there in the street, but the hesitation made my reply seem insincere. She groaned, "*Ya, Allah,*" throwing up her hands and forgetting me.

I went to the press then and persuaded both the owner and the shop foreman that my little brochure was urgent and the typesetting absolutely had to be done by Saturday. I drank coffee. We laughed once. I mentioned meeting a woman whose son was kidnapped. They shrugged.

"That's the way it is these days," the shop foreman said. "Maybe he was a communist, or maybe somebody didn't like him."

The man at the photo shop promised his "best effort" to get my pictures ready by noon Saturday. He added something I missed, because I was thinking about my son looking for his future on some unknown highway, his sleeping bag strapped behind him on the motorcycle.

On the way back up the hill on this most beautiful day of the year, I found that I had gotten through the army checkpoint without knowing and caught myself saying, "They will kill him," and beating the steering-wheel with my hands.

Nadia in the Shelter

I sit here wondering. While the world explodes, my mother groans and the radio blares martial music, I sit here wondering what Hagob is thinking: that all luck has run out? That the last good person in the world has given up the effort? Or died under the shells?

The main difference now between us and the rats is that we wonder about the rest of the world. The candle on the floor throws our distorted shadows on the walls. My brother fidgets, wiggling his fingers, bouncing his knees, so his shadow wiggles and bounces, and Mother snaps at him, "Can't you be still for one minute?" Their eyes are dark hollows in the dimness. As always, I sit on this little box, hunched over, hugging my legs to keep from leaning on the cold wall. We hear the booms, glance at one another, look away quickly and wonder. Newsflashes interrupt the battle music. With fascination and dread, we listen to the names of the dead and wounded. (Once Marwan said, "I have to hear the casualty list to be sure I'm not on it." It was very funny at the time.)

Surely Hagob realizes nobody with good sense would get in a car and go down to the Green Line today. It was hard enough to do all these months. Even after listening every time to the news to make sure there was nothing happening, I would start out with half a heart of courage. Then I would see the barricades—big metal containers piled along the edge of the street, so people could walk behind them without being visible to snipers. The good paved street would dribble away into broken asphalt and dust, and all my good intentions would drain out through my legs.

Hagob's building is at the very edge of no man's land, the last one with any clean, straight lines. The next one, like all those beyond, has all the corners and edges knocked off and pockmarks and gaping holes in the walls. They look like something spongy and rotten that has been eaten by a monstrous mouse.

(Right now I don't know whether I'm holding my breath because of this memory of silence and stillness in a dead city or because of the shell whistling over our heads.)

Always at that point in the street I would get a good case of chicken skin, as we say in French, those little chill bumps, even when the day was warm and sunny and a shot hadn't been fired in six months. There were times when I backed out of the street, just because I didn't see another car going that way. And then I got home and felt guilty that I had left Hagob sitting there expectantly, with a bottled drink, bought for me, cooling in the little refrigerator, the television screen black, and with nothing to do with his anger. I would listen to the news again. Had there been any shooting? To give me a reason, to prove I was wise, not spineless.

But usually I got there. To be fair to myself, yes, I usually did. As soon as I found a parking place and got under the shadow of the building I felt better. Hagob lives (lived?) on the seventh floor. There is an ancient elevator, small and jerky, the kind from which the walls of the shaft are visible, moving past in a coarse, gray blur. I never use it. When by chance there is electricity, I feel sure it will go off the instant I start up. (Rescuing people out of elevators is a common art in Beirut. Marwan once told me—everything makes me think of Marwan, though the pictures of him in my head tend to fade like very old photographs—that the average time necessary was sixteen minutes. Probably our skill has increased since then from lots of practice.) Once I walked down, arriving at the second floor just in time to see two girls step into the elevator. The iron grill closed behind them, and up they went. By the time I was going out through the main door of the building, I could hear them pounding and screaming up there between floors. I laughed, because I was free.

Sometimes I feel cocky, like I live because I'm smart. I'm not Phoenician for nothing. And then a shell hits a wall and I go out and find that big stones have crushed the car in front of mine and the car behind, and I know that's not how I live.

My legs are strong from climbing the stairs of apartment buildings, except when they are weak because I'm a coward. In some buildings I have to go up slowly when there's no electricity, with one hand pointing my little flashlight at the dark step in front of me and the other hand on the wall. I can't believe how black it is in those stairwells, and I'm terrified of touching a spider or meeting a cockroach. But Hagob's building is a cheap one, with an open stairwell, drafty and cold in winter, but light. The stairwell is also on the protected side of the building, facing another inhabited apartment house. As I climb I can see into all the kitchens of the other building. One kitchen has red curtains and a maid from Sri Lanka, and the next one up has broken blinds, always hanging on a slant, and a woman with a tired face, who seems to live at the sink, staring through her dingy window at Hagob's stairwell. The smells tell their own story—garlic and frying potatoes and chicken boiling with cinnamon. I usually get there around noon, a bit shaky with hunger.

Trudging up and down, with my big bag hanging from one shoulder, I often wonder about the people in those kitchens, what kind of texture life has to a woman far from home in someone else's kitchen or to another growing gray at her own sink in the madness of Ain arRommaneh. And sometimes I wonder what they think when they see a girl in jeans climbing the stairs at the same time every Wednesday. Do they know which apartment I go to and what my business is there? Does it show on my face that I spend most of my time in drab and hidden rooms where people are trapped in their broken bodies? Do these strangers ever think, like some of my friends, "If that girl didn't climb all those stairs, she might not be so skinny"?

My friends know that if this girl didn't see so many people who can't climb the stairs, or move their bowels or scratch their own noses, she might not be so cautious. Mr Jabri, for instance, got shot at the Green Line, just coming home from work one afternoon. The bullet burned through only half his spinal cord, so that he has feeling without movement on one side of his body and movement without feeling on the other. (Some of our tragedies seem created by miracles.) I did what I could for him, stretching his muscles, moving his joints, teaching him how things work. He wanted so badly to walk, and he can now, exactly like Frankenstein walks. They have a daily horror show in that house.

You never know when it will happen. A rifle shot will echo among the tall buildings and sound like six. The bullet will ricochet and sing; a person hit will wonder why he is bleeding.

To some people, it happens as it did to Marwan. Between a chance meeting in the afternoon, a chance that made us laugh, and our date in the evening, a shell took him so that, at first, my loss bore the marks of an appointment not kept. My little brother teased me, "Your sweetie didn't come."

Micho was just a little kid then, not this lanky teenager who's bouncing his knee again and arguing with my mother.

At the time I thought anything would have been better than what happened, even a half-life in which we could not get married, or even walk together anymore, down on the lower road, under the snobar trees. I could sit by his bed; I could hold his hand; maybe we could talk. But later I had a patient who could move nothing but his eyelids, and I decided I was wrong. Marwan would have died again in his spirit every morning. We would have been prisoners, both of us.

Hagob can walk with a cane, very slowly. I haven't done much for him, really. I don't know why he thinks I'm so good. I brought him the cane, from an organization that lends them indefinitely. When he doesn't need it, he's supposed to send it back, but of course, he won't get better. I stretch his clenched fingers a little, without hope. I take his blood pressure. Stroke victims always keep worrying about their blood pressure. Once I called a doctor, when it was too high.

In principle I try to give priority to cases that will improve, though I get the most hopeless problems, but in Hagob's case the issue is no longer the improvement of the patient. Sometimes I ask myself what the issue really is.

I'm not attached to him. I don't get attached to my patients, except sometimes to old ladies, who are sweet and make up ailments to keep me coming. I have learned to defend myself by keeping a certain distance. Now I neither think about them when I am away nor dread going back to them, though I used to actually hate them—for having bed sores, for smelling bad, for depending on people instead of trying, and for thinking they were the only people who suffer. Nobody prepared me for that when I was studying physical therapy. Nobody taught me that these paralyzed people could be stubborn beyond reason.

I catch myself in a contradiction here. I say I do not think about my patients, but I am thinking about Hagob. Mother is trying to talk to me, and I am off in Ain arRommaneh. She needs to go to the bathroom and is afraid; Micho is hungry. And already my legs are getting numb. It always astounds me how quickly a shelter becomes a jail.

Hagob sits there all day, facing the front door, in a room not much bigger than a closet. All day I zigzag through the poorest parts of the city in my decrepit car. (I got the shrapnel holes filled and proofed against rust, but I can't afford a paint job, so now I have a blue car with white polka dots. The cover over the horn falls off when I turn corners. Marwan would have loved it.) Wherever I go, I pass some little grocery with awnings, faded green, and boxes of vegetables on the sidewalk. I usually fall into a hole in the street like the one in front of Baz's brass shop or Shouky's garage, and smell *chawarma* as I near a sandwich stand. Around me the crowds mill and dart and carry loads and shout and gesture and struggle. Then, when I get to the seventh floor of the last building in civilization, it is a dark and shabby room, a cage.

The first time I saw him, he was alone and staring. He occupied the chair like a stone, his thickness sinking into the upholstery and springs, his hands heavy on the armrests.

I explained, "Your wife called and asked me to come."

He said, "Hunh!", a sound quietly contemptuous.

I said, "Let me see you move your arms."

He said, "For what?" with his blunt face full of bitterness and suspicion.

"Because I need to know what you can do."

He said, "We don't have any money."

I said, "Money isn't the question. The question is, Do you want to live?"

And the muscles hardened at the corner of his jaw.

If Hagob had been hit by a faceless sniper or a car bomb that no one claimed credit for, I would have understood his rage, but something failed in his body. No one could prevent it. I wonder sometimes if he realizes that this country is sick with anger, that there is a plague, and he is only one of many.

Every week it's the same. I open the door, and he is staring at the bare walls or the dead television. The book I offered him last time is where I left it, with one week of dust on the jacket. The Bible he has never read is still on a little shelf high up in the corner. But the anger behind his eyes withdraws slightly, because I have come.

He always urges me to sit on the small couch beside his chair. I tend to perch on the edge, because its back is the wall, and I cannot lean so far. Sometimes the tumbled sheet on the couch reminds me that it is really someone's bed I am sitting on and not a very clean bed. (Actually this house is clean, one of the cleanest I go to, but I am squeamish about contact with people's beds.) From the couch I look into the other room, where three single beds stand in a row and an old washing machine serves as a table. The stack of clothes on top of the machine probably means that there is no closet in the room. They have two teenaged boys, and I wonder if it is Hagob or his wife who sleeps on the couch, but it is none of my business.

When I try to move his stiff leg, to keep a little flexibility in the knee, it is heavy and lifeless, like a log. The expression on his face does not move any more quickly. Even the white fringe around his bald head is always the same, as though it doesn't grow.

We have certain communication problems, Hagob and I. His Arabic is broken and his speech a bit slurred. Since he is uneducated, too, French and English don't help. I actually don't know his family name, a strange Armenian name; he tells me and I miss it every time. But I understand enough to know that he tells me things I don't need to hear.

His wife works as a cleaning woman. Sometimes she arrives home while I am there. We can hear her shoes slapping against the stairs for a long time, and then she shuffles in, out of breath, and they begin shouting at each other. Other times she doesn't come, and he says to me at about one o'clock, "She works from eight to twelve. What does she do from twelve to two?"

I say, "Maybe they delayed her, or maybe she's buying vegetables."

And he says, "She is a prostitute." I was shocked the first time.

His wife has red hair and blue eyes and freckles on her face and arms. She is slender, though at first I thought she was four months pregnant, because of her belly, but she has been that way for six months. Her hands feel like sandpaper; the nails are stained in the cracks. She works in broken shoes and always the same dress, worn so thin it may soon disintegrate.

They yap at each other in Armenian, which I don't understand, except for the rising tone of anger. At the peak of this tone they always break into Arabic. Arabic must be the world's best language in which to be angry.

She calls him, "Stroke." She says, "What did you do while I was scrubbing floors, Stroke? Did you earn a kilo of bread? Did you make chicken and rice for our lunch? Did the president call to ask your opinion?"

"Watch your tongue, woman," he shouts. "I don't take insults from an unclean woman."

"He is useless," she says to me, in front of him. "He was always useless. Do you know when he had the stroke? Two years ago. Do you know how many years I carried water up these stairs? Ten years. Do you know how we got the pump? I put it. I mopped floors to buy it, so I won't break my back and quit like him."

I try not to say anything. I go to the kitchen and wash my hands. It is a cramped and ugly kitchen but clean. She never leaves dishes in the sink.

Sometimes they curse. I am shy even to remember such words. Once I was so upset that I shouted, too. I said, "Shame on you for talking like this in front of me."

Suddenly they fell quiet.

Another time they shouted so much a neighbor came, a nice lady with kind eyes and a sympathetic voice. She said to me, "She has a hard time, because of this man."

After that I tried to talk to Hagob more. I told him, "God loves you," risking a contemptuous smirk. (Once when Jenny said that to me, only courtesy prevented my laughing. Hatred was written on the walls of the world and falling from the sky in random disasters. Marwan was dead. In those days it was my anger that gave a kind of meaning to things. But eventually it made a difference—not realizing that they were loved, my stubborn patients and the people who shoot at us, but realizing that I was loved.)

I encouraged Hagob to pray, thinking it would occupy some time and make him softer. Now when he tells me bad stories about how tough his life is, he lifts his heavy fist slowly toward the ceiling and says, "I tell him. He knows how they treat me." When his wife isn't there, he still talks about her. He tells me that she doesn't feed him properly. "She cooks for the boys. They have meat and vegetables. She gives me bread and yogurt."

This could be true. They probably don't have enough food, and growing boys have to eat.

Before his stroke he made coffee at a little coffee house and carried it to people in offices all over the neighborhood. I try to imagine him in a soiled apron, stirring the coffee into the pot with his big hands, balancing two little cups of coffee and two glasses of water on a tray, crossing the street on his tree-trunk legs, between moving cars. That was his job. As far as I know, that's all he knows how to do. Now he can't even make himself a cup of coffee. He can't stand without the cane.

I got them a box of food from our church. One of the fellows helped me deliver it, because I couldn't lift the box. Zahi carried it up the seven flights of stairs, without stopping. "It's nothing," he claimed, but he got big drops of sweat on his face. (Marwan would have staggered and pretended he was collapsing, just for a laugh.)

It was the only time I saw Hagob look surprised. He was surprised and pleased about the box of food, surprised and pleased about this stalwart young visitor, who said, "I'm glad to meet you, sir," and "How is your health?" and "Sir, can I do anything for you before I go?"

Afterwards Zahi was very friendly with me. He said, "I enjoyed going with you, Nadia. Let me help you again sometime." But I think I shut the door by some coolness in my voice.

The next time I went to see Hagob he said, "You are the last good person in the world. There aren't any more."

Guilt hit me, as it does sometimes, like a little sting or an itch. I said, "But it was my church that sent the food. It was Zahi who carried it up the stairs."

"Because of you, Nadia. I know."

In no way does he get any better, but he wants me to come, and I can't think of a way to stop. He is grateful. Wednesday at noon he sees someone "good". I ask myself, must I go so that Hagob will not be disillusioned? Do I go because I still need to think I am good?

In the summer one or both of the boys would be there sometimes when I came. He would ask one of them to open the drink in the refrigerator for me. I would protest sincerely, because I can't bear drinking sugar on an empty stomach and would have a headache if I did, but the boy would open it, as his father said, his hair falling in his eyes as he bent over the bottle, his trousers loose and unpressed. I would swallow a little and put it down and talk, trying to give the impression that I completely forgot to drink it.

"I heard some amazing news today, Hagob. They're tearing down the Berlin Wall. People spent the night knocking holes in it with hammers and chisels."

"They don't need that wall anymore?"

"It divides the city, like our Green Line, you know, except worse."

"Do they shoot across it?"

"Well, not since a long time ago, I think."

"Congratulations to them. Nobody is shooting. Drink your cola, Nadia."

"Oh, yes, my drink," tilting a few drops into my mouth, feeling nauseous. "Thank you, Hagob."

I sit there holding the cool, sticky bottle. "I want you to walk around more, Hagob. It's important for your heart and lungs."

"I try, Nadia, but they leave things in my way—chairs and shoes and schoolbooks. They want me to fall down."

"Nonsense. They just forget. I really need to go now. I'll just put this bottle in the kitchen for you." As I said this one day, I raised it to my lips, and when I was out of sight I poured the sweet liquid down the sink, feeling terrible about wasting what he couldn't afford.

Such a silly and important game we played. And when I looked into the bedroom where the boy went as soon as he had done his duty about the drink, and lifted a hand to tell him goodbye, I found his face impassive but could feel that he understood: both Hagob and I had lost the game. On the way home for lunch I thought about it and knew in my cynical center that boys grow up already angry and proud and play the same games their fathers played.

In winter, when the boys were not there, he frequently told me they were worthless. "They fail in school. I try to make them study, and they just ignore me. I am nothing. They see me as nothing. What can I do? Get up and beat them? They don't respect me. I disgust them. They wish I would die."

It won't help to tell Hagob that most of my patients think like that. Because they feel useless, they think everyone wants them dead. Hagob would agree. Maybe he understands that his paralysis paralyzes them all, though he is wrong about the reasons.

He smolders until he thinks of his wife; then he bursts into flames. "Immoral woman! I don't know why I married her. It was her idea. She came to this house and enticed me to marry her."

I don't know what to believe. The woman smells like sweat and kerosene. She walks all the way down to Bourj Hammoud to get his medicine free from the Armenians. I wonder what Marwan would have said about these two. Probably that Hagob with his wife is a pot that found its lid.

Hagob's view of the world is the flat gray roofs of Ain arRommaneh, cluttered with water tanks and television aerials. I wonder if he knows anymore how snobar trees along the top of a hill look like little umbrellas, daylight showing under their branches, or if he can remember an expanse of shining water on which ships glide away, shrinking and fading until they disappear into the blue blur of sea and sky. He has not been out of doors or in the sun or down the stairs for two years. He will not go until he is carried out dead. Until one of his anger fits pushes him to a heart attack, unless he has been hit already by an artillery shell.

I understand from experience that anger is all he has. It is his barricade against grief. But this barricade traps the one it defends. Only those who mourn can be comforted.

For three years I didn't cry about Marwan or talk about him or call his parents or speak to God. There was nothing official between us. We need a license to care in this country, so no one knew my feelings for him. And afterwards no one knew how much I dreaded living, how long and useless it all seemed. Probably people noticed that I got a sharp tongue and didn't go out of my way for anybody, and worse things maybe. But my friend Jenny kept saying, "Nadia, God loves you." And, though I didn't notice any connection, one day, without planning to, I told her about Marwan. It started easy, just a story about a guy I used to know, this witty, natural sort of a guy who could make me silly happy just by saying "Hi."

He was taking me to a party one evening and that afternoon I went shopping for a gift, and on a crowded sidewalk I poked somebody in the head with one of the little spokes of my umbrella, and it was Marwan. I even told her how he got under the umbrella with me, and his eyes were level with mine and crinkled with laughter. It was nothing, but it seemed a very intimate thing to be telling, especially to say that I was so happy suddenly that I was afraid. (Already then we were afraid to be happy.) I told her that half an hour later a shell fell on Ashrafiyeh, on Marwan, who was ten meters from his own door. I meant to describe how I sat waiting in the evening, holding the umbrella, and how my brother teased me; and in the telling of it I felt for an instant worthless and unwanted and mad because he didn't come, and knew that I was going to cry at last. And I shut my eyes and tried not to and said, "I didn't cry when it happened. It's so silly to cry now." And the tears came. And came and came and wouldn't stop.

For weeks after I let down my defenses, all sorts of garbage came leaping through the breach, and I cried because of what some kid said about my glasses when I was twelve and because I lost my youth somewhere under the shells and couldn't remember when. And other things, even old ladies with broken hips, slipped inside somehow, and love from unexpected directions, and I started waking up in the morning ecstatic about the sunrise and scared, scared of snipers, scared that something might steal my adulthood too. Or maybe it was God I was afraid of losing.

So many times since then, I've almost embarrassed myself. Everybody is raging and acting cynical, and I am on the verge of hugging somebody or weeping. I have to get up and say tough words, and clatter the coffee cups and slam the doors so people will know this is still Nadia.

I guess all that is the explanation for why I am a softy and contradictory and cowardly and haven't been to see Hagob in weeks or stopped thinking about him. There were times I might have gone, but I couldn't know the lull would last so long. Once I started to go. I was halfway to Mkalles when I heard a newsflash. Shells were falling in Sin el Fil.

Maybe he is angry at me, even me. I think that he cannot afford to be angry at me, and suddenly I can imagine how anger is going to rise up in his throat so thick and fierce it will choke him. He will try in vain to get his hands to his collar to pull death away.

As soon as the shells stop falling, I will try again. Maybe I will have the courage to go all the way. There won't be any traffic, so I could drive on the wrong side of the street close to the barricades. (I'm getting chicken skin just thinking about it.)

Please let it not be too late. I need to admit to him that I am a coward, that I didn't come for so long because I was afraid of getting hurt in the street and being helpless like him. I will tell him about Marwan and about being angry for so long. Oh no. This is not easy. What will I do if he starts talking and talking, what if he remembers what I suspect—that he loved her once and meant to be a good husband?

It must be a wretched thing to look back and know you've bungled your life, worse than thinking you were robbed, worse even than looking forward and seeing an empty desert.

Jenny once said to me, "There are other young men, aren't there? Marriage is still a possibility." She said it, knowing that a single woman is nobody (except to herself), and in spite of knowing how difficult everything has become, how few weddings we have in this country.

I said, "Maybe, but not really." And I looked away from her eyes and added, "Anyway, I don't want to dream about it."

Micho has taken off his shoes, and Mother is complaining that his socks stink. Actually the air is getting very stale in here; I feel as feeble as this candle. An empty silence has fallen, and we are caught in that uncertain period near the end of a battle. It always makes me think of being in a sailboat when the wind dies.

Probably I should stick to physical therapy. Who am I to make Hagob remember? He stares, as though there were nothing in the world but walls. And I back out of relationships with the same panic that I back away from the no man's land. Still, it proves my point. We are not, any of us, good or useful, but we are loved anyway. And isn't it one choice we can make, to die of our anger or not?

Actually, there is hope for Hagob. And now that the guns are quiet, I feel like escaping, like doing something really wild. I think I'll ask Zahi to round up a couple of his biggest friends to help me carry Hagob down the stairs. If we can carry him out dead, we can carry him out alive. Zahi will insist it's "no problem." Hagob will protest, making the guys look like kidnappers. It'll be a carnival (if we don't spill him); the neighbors will come out and make suggestions and a big commotion. We'll get him into the car somehow and haul him off to the beach.

Zahi will probably grab onto some wrong idea from my invitation, and I'll be jumpy all the time, fretting that maybe the cease-fire won't hold, but this is an emergency. I can see it now: only fire trucks and ambulances on the road and a polka-dotted getaway car with the rear end dragging, roaring and clanking down the *autostrad*, rushing a reluctant escapee out to look at the horizon, and his faint and suffocating friend to smell the sea.

Susie and Saeed

The only thing Susie liked more than motorcycles was cute boys who owned motorcycles. Well, maybe she liked airplanes more than motorcycles and would one day come unglued over good-looking pilots, but the summer she was seventeen the most we had to worry about was motorcycles and Saeed.

On a sultry afternoon in June Saeed roared into our lives. It was the kind of day in which Susie did not usually have fun at the swimming pool because every kid who could swim and half of those who couldn't would be there. "There isn't room to get wet," she used to complain. Yet she went, probably in hope that some good-looking Lebanese boy would bring her home on his motorcycle.

When I heard the rumble and sputter downstairs I went right on popping ice cubes out of the plastic tray and pouring tea over them. I sliced a lemon, flinching once with the knife in my hand, because the machine backfired as it revved up to leave. I guess it didn't really sound like gunfire, but I tend to be jittery.

A moment later I heard Susie running up the stairs, her clogs clattering past the doors of our neighbors. She fumbled at the lock so long that I opened the door for her, noticing immediately that her face was burned and that something nice must have happened.

"Mom," she said, "I'm so excited." She had a large book under her left elbow, a bathing suit in her hand and an enormous green beach towel over her shoulder.

"Let me hang up this stuff and I'll tell you all the juicy details. Ummm. Got some more of that tea?"

Coming into the kitchen, still breathless, she said, "I met the cutest guy in the whole world. Mom, I promise you I've never seen anybody so adorable. His name is Saeed, and he has a Honda 750."

"Is that who brought you home?"

"Brought me home! He took me for this fantastic ride down a little back road through a snobar forest. Man, the way he rides that bike!"

She was leaning against the cupboard drinking her tea and munching crackers, a chubby seventeen-year-old in faded jeans and a cotton smock, her pink face animated and happy. Then she put down the glass so she could talk with her hands. "We went zagging through the traffic, between the cars, and then zipping down the hill, with the trees flying past, and we were leaning way over into the curves. Oh, it was great. I've never had so much fun!"

Her red hair had blown into a dry tangle, and her cheeks were getting pinker.

"You got sunburned," I told her.

She said, "It was worth it," and then went on chattering. "He's just like a little boy. You know? Sort of funny, even when he's serious. And his English is terrible, so terrible that it's wonderful. He said to me, 'I'm sorry I speak bad language.'" She imitated his tense consonants and heavy "r" sounds. "And when I told him that I would give him English lessons, he said, 'You are very dangerous.'" She stopped to giggle. "I couldn't figure out what he meant, so I told him to say it in Arabic, and you know what he was trying to say? Generous! He wanted to say, 'You are very generous.' Because I smiled, he got worried and asked me, 'What did I speak?' And I told him and then we just cracked up."

She laughed while telling it, wobbling weakly and wiping her eyes. Suddenly she sighed heavily and looked almost pained as she said, "He has long eyelashes, and they curl up to here."

I asked a few pertinent questions about Saeed, but she didn't know any of the answers.

"Well, really, Mom, when you're just getting to know a guy you don't ask boring questions like where do you work or personal questions like how old are you and which militia group are you in."

All evening we heard about Saeed, his cute manners and funny expressions, his pretty muscles. "What a bod!" she said. "I couldn't believe it."

Her brother Rick, who was two years older and a sophomore in college, sat with his head bent over his guitar as he strummed quietly. He looked up and said, "I don't know how you do it, Susie. Last summer suave Samir, this summer Mr Universe."

And their father said, "Rick, please, I have lived nine happy months without hearing that joker's name."

But Susie was already laughing. "At least don't put Saeed in the same category as Samir. Nobody else is that worthless." And with a toss of her head she laughed off the mistakes of last summer.

In spite of her slightly mad crazes and crushes, or maybe because of them, it was usually Susie who saved us from taking life too seriously. She had just graduated from the American Academy in Athens, where we had sent her because of the war in Lebanon, and in Athens she had decided to be an aeronautical engineer. Being surprised by Susie was the only part of the decision that didn't surprise us.

Rick had forfeited a summer job in Boston so that we could all be at home again in Lebanon, and as soon as they arrived the civil war began to flare up again here and there all over the country, as if by spontaneous combustion. It was a fragile time both for us and for Lebanon. We stayed close to home, made a lot of ice cream and shish kabob on the balcony, watched the lavender reflections of sunsets against the eastern mountains, and hoped the battles would stay somewhere down the road at least until September.

At the supper table that night Susie mentioned that before the war Saeed used to do stunt shows on his motorcycle, jumping over big metal drums and then cars.

And Rick said, "Oh, I know him. I mean I used to see him around. His bike has four-in-one headers and two fog passing lights on the front. Right? Well, I think you ought to know that he usually has a certain girl hanging on behind him and she just happens to be out of the country right now."

Susie's hazel eyes were suddenly defensive. "So?"

"So don't get all..."

"Look, I know about Allison. She's the principal's secretary at the high school, sort of his assistant actually, and she's in London for the summer. Does that mean I can't go riding with Saeed?"

And her father said, "I'm not as worried about Allison as I am about Evel Knievel. I can't get excited about your riding with a stunt man."

"Oh, Dad, he doesn't show off on the road!"

And Rick redeemed himself by saying, "Actually, he's an incredible motorcyclist. I think he's always in control."

While we were discussing the next day's schedule she announced that she had to hang loose because Saeed might come, and once she interrupted a comfortable silence in the living room to say dreamily, "On a scale of one to ten, I give him fourteen."

Rick's dark eyes appealed to me to do something. All I did was marvel to myself; Susie's happiness is perpetually out on a limb.

After Susie had spent several afternoons with Saeed, I sent him an invitation to dinner, partly to find out for myself who Saeed was. In spite of all the advance introduction I was a little surprised when I saw him. He looked so small as he walked in, carrying a monstrous black helmet under his left arm, and his big eyes were astonishingly green in his suntanned face.

Susie's face was shining. She said, "Hey, guys, this is Saeed. Saeed, this is my mom Jenny, my brother Rick, and my dad. He's Roger."

He shook hands with each of us quickly, saying "hello" three times in a shy voice. Then he ran his fingers through a heap of rough, disorderly hair, straightening it a bit on his high forehead and around his ears. He was very neat and clean, in tight blue jeans and zippered boots. When he took off his windbreaker he looked bigger, because his chest and biceps bulged under a knit shirt. He was as compact and hard as a clenched fist.

Roger began repeating all the proper Arabic assurances of welcome, and Susie and I went to the kitchen to pour the tea and put the food in the dishes. She said, "Oh, I hope he likes everything."

When I went in to call them to the dining-room, Saeed and Rick were discussing motorcycles in a clumsy mixture of English and Arabic. Saeed jumped up to demonstrate his riding form and said, "I make like this, and we fly over the cars."

The five of us occupied only half of our large dining table, Roger at one end, Susie and I on the side nearer the kitchen, Saeed and Rick opposite us. A plate of cornbread, cut into yellow squares, was just in front of Saeed. He picked it up and said, "It's cake?"

Rick told him, "It's *khubz*."

"We eat it now?" He put a piece on his plate before passing it to Rick. Then he watched from the corner of his eye, curious and concerned, as Rick, according to his own peculiar habit, cut a hole in the top of his square of cornbread and filled the hole with butter and honey. Saeed imitated him, obviously relieved that he had so quickly mastered the art of eating this strange bread.

Once he looked across the table at Susie and when their eyes met a sudden brilliant smile flashed across his face. Then he grew serious, the muscles squirming in his long jaw. I thought that Susie had not exaggerated anything. Those extravagant eyelashes, together with green eyes and olive skin, gave him a truly dramatic face. Then I noticed for the first time his arrogant, crooked nose and the scar that interrupted one of his eyebrows. Hollywood would have loved Saeed in a handsome gangster role.

"What you do in Lubnan?" he asked us.

And Roger explained, "Jenny works part-time with a publisher, and I teach in the American University. This spring I managed to get transferred to the new branch on this side of the Green Line."

"It's better for you," Saeed said. "Maybe the sniper he not shoot you and you going to work."

Though he was serious, we all laughed.

"I, too, come to this side," he said, "because better for me, and I don't fight in this war, because I have many friends, Muslim friends, on the other side, and anyway I don't want to make these dirty things."

When he said, "dirty," he flipped his small hands as though shaking off something filthy.

"And before the war," he went on, "I become Christian. I mean, not like I have Christian on my I.D. only, but like I... what you say? I chose? Yes, I chose, because I believe, and I think it's not for Christians to kill people."

Susie turned to me, the curve of her eyebrows going up, as though to say, "An interesting answer to your question!"

Saeed was saying, "You don't know how dirty is this war. Oooof! This killing!" He shook his hands again. "Many times they ask me, al Kata'ib and al Ahrar, why I don't fight with them, and sometimes they angry from me, but I pray and my God he help me and thanks God I live and don't kill anybody."

Susie had made a fancy chocolate dessert, and when she served it Saeed covered his flat abdomen with both hands and said, "Oooof! It's big."

Roger said, "Why is mine smaller than Saeed's?"

And Susie said, "Because you are fatter than Saeed."

Roger took a swing at the seat of her jeans and said, "Smarty-pants!"

Saeed looked up quickly, his forehead wrinkled, and said, "Smarty-pants? What? What's the meaning of smarty-pants?"

And Susie said, "Oh, Dad, see what you did."

"It's not good—smarty-pants?" Saeed twisted his hand in a questioning gesture.

Explaining smarty-pants in Arabic proved to be quite a challenge. After several abortive efforts Roger told him, "It means *ashtar min laazim.*"

Rick and I looked at one another in surprise and said in unison, "Smarter than necessary?" Then we all laughed.

With a gentle and amused smile on his wide mouth, Saeed looked at Susie again and said, "It's a good name. Smarty-pants. Susie Smarty-pants."

Susie blushed but laughed her frank and urgent laughter. "Why am I the one who gets all these crazy nicknames?"

Then Saeed told us, "I want to learn well the English, because I leave school when I'm thirteen, and my father he drunk, and in the school the teacher hitted me, so I run away. And I want to ride the motorbike, so I work and eat only bread and hummus and I save all my money 'til I buy the motorbike. And I become better than anybody in Lubnan on the motorbike, because I live on her. She become like my house.

"But now, because of the war nobody pay me to ride the bike, only Mr Wakim. I work for Pharmacy Wakim, and I take the medicine to the people when they call. And I have a girlfriend. She's British, but she don't like to help me with the English. She works, and she say she already tired, when she see me and she want to have fun. Even I do mistakes in the Arabic.

"I want to make something with my life, but now how I study? Because I become old for the school, and if I not study in the school I never have good work. You think if I go to America, maybe I get good work?"

Roger told him, "Well, in America many people don't have a job."

"It's also very hard to get a visa," I added.

He turned to Rick then and asked him, "What you study in college?"

"Maybe computer science."

"Oh, it's good. You will have good job and take much money."

Rick smiled and his glance toward me was only a flick of his eyelids. He was not sure he knew what to study, but this uncertainty had been ignored and he was glad. He said, "I hope so."

Then Saeed looked at Susie. "And you? What will you study in California?"

"Aeronautical engineering."

"Air-o what?" He looked to Roger for an explanation.

After Roger translated aeronautical engineering into Arabic, Saeed just sat staring at Susie, his lips slightly open, the upward sweep of those gorgeous eyelashes adding to an expression of surprise. Then he dropped his eyes for a moment, closed his mouth tight and began to nod slowly. "Smarty-pants," he said and then flashed at her that white, lopsided smile.

Before he left we all promised to help him by correcting his English, and Roger gave him some simple books to read, which he zipped into his windbreaker. I invited him to come often, using an Arabic expression, "The house is your house."

Outside our door, standing at the top of the stairs, a tough, handsome little boy with a huge black helmet in his hands, he said, "You are a very kind and dangerous family," and fled down the stairs.

After that he adopted us, the way a homeless puppy adopts himself a family. We all knew the sound of his motorcycle and would shout, "Saeed is here!" And someone would drop a key off the balcony so he could get into the building. Almost every day in the late afternoon he would take Susie for a ride. There was often fighting in parts of Beirut and in some villages higher up the mountain, but I felt they were safe in our area of the hills above the city, and I knew that Saeed had a dread of the roadblocks they would confront if they left the vicinity. Rick would go along on his 350, and they would ride through the pretty mountain towns, waving at people they knew, stopping at shaded roadside cafés for soft drinks and ice cream, and exploring the small curving roads that wound between granite boulders and umbrella pines.

Saeed's employer had given him the use of a room over the pharmacy, but he obviously didn't go there until he had run out of alternatives. Sometimes he visited his mother in a suburb of Beirut. He ate with us so often that I got used to putting five plates on the table in the evenings.

He usually came with his English book zipped into his windbreaker and after supper someone would listen to him read and explain a word or a construction he didn't understand. He began to use many new words, not always accurately.

Once he told me that Allison "complicated" him. I simply waited to find out exactly what that meant.

I often wondered if his English was helped or hindered by being with Susie and Rick, because the three of them developed a humorous language of their own, an intimate blending of colloquial

Arabic and English grammar, and jazzy American slang with poetic Arabic expressions. They went riding on the *"motorcycletain,"* and if they were just going to cruise through Broummana to see who was in the streets, they would say, "Mom, we're going *kizdiring*." When they were preparing for a trip into the canyon below us, I heard Susie say, *"Yalla,* let's hit the twisties, *ya shabab."*

One day Rick said, "This is a new language. We have to give it a name. What can we call it?"

"How about *lugat al insane*?" Susie said.

"Or something like Arabeng."

Ideas began exploding like popcorn. Engelarab led to jinglearab, slangarab, arabglish, arabish, engelbic. Each proposal brought new laughter. Finally Susie and Rick narrowed the choices to Engelarab and Arabish and asked Saeed to choose between them. He chose Arabish and kept saying it over and over as though he loved the sound of it. After that something which usually happens spontaneously was deliberate, and the language spoken in our house became more and more preposterous.

Looking back I realize that we all lived that summer as though it would last forever. Rick was struggling with a personal confusion about what country he belonged to and what to do with his life, and Roger and I didn't even want to wonder when we would have our children in Lebanon again. Susie apparently pretended that Allison would never be back. As for Saeed, he acted as though he would always be one of us, though one night he must have been thinking of Allison when he said, "I think Americans are more friendly than the British."

"What makes you think that?" we asked him.

"Well, Mrs Chapman, Allison's mother, she don't like me coming to their house. She tell me I come too much, and she let me eat there only if she invite me special. And one time she become very angry from me, because Allison, she tell me I don't want to see you every day. You can't come 'til Saturday. But I couldn't wait 'til Saturday. It was long time, and so I climb by the post up to her balcony, and I enter her room. Then she shout at me and Mrs

Chapman hear us and she become very angry from me."

All of us listened to this story in silent amazement.

"After that," he went on, "I see Mrs Chapman in the street, and I make like this at her..." He lifted his hand as in greeting.

"You waved," Susie prompted him.

"Yes, I wave, and she don't speak to me." Lifting his big shoulders and turning his palms up, he said, "She act like she don't know me."

"But, Saeed," Roger said, "most people would be upset if a man climbed into their daughter's window."

"But Allison, she is my special friend," he said. "She must not to tell me I can't come."

And Rick said, rather slowly and carefully, "Well, if a girl tells me not to come until Saturday, I just make myself wait until Saturday."

It began to worry me that Saeed was so young at twenty-five, but when I mentioned this to Roger, he said, "Well, yes, but on the other hand he has made some really hard decisions and stood by them. Not fighting in the war, for instance. The pressure to participate must be really tough."

He was right, of course, and I was eager to believe only the best about Saeed.

One Saturday night the young people were invited to a party in a nearby town. Rick drove our car, so they left the motorcycles parked by the gate. Roger and I went to bed early and lay quietly, enjoying a soft breeze from the sea. In the patio below our bedroom some neighbors were playing backgammon. We could hear the clicking of the dice and occasional laughter. Then somewhere down the hill there was the abrupt stutter of a machine gun. And silence. Then a machine gun again. We said nothing. We listened. Several machine guns began to speak at once.

Roger rolled over and said, "Where did those kids go?"

"To Mansourieh, but I don't know whose house."

A big explosion shook the darkness.

"Can you tell where that is?" I asked him.

He got up and stood on the balcony and listened. The machine guns rattled. The neighbors were talking excitedly down in the yard. He came back inside and said, "The way the hills echo the sounds, I can't be sure, but I think it's farther down the hill than Mansourieh."

Unable to sleep but trying not to imagine the worst, we filled the time talking about Susie and Saeed. Wasn't she just glowing more and more every day, I wondered.

Roger said the end of summer would take care of it.

"In a rather cruel way," I added. "You know what bothers me? We all encouraged her. By falling for Saeed ourselves, inviting him to dinner, teaching him English, letting him practically live here."

There was another explosion down the hill.

"I wish they would at least call us."

Roger said, "Probably all the trunk lines are busy. Besides, there'll be one phone in the house and everybody at the party wanting to use it."

They came home soon, a little disappointed, studiously blasé.

"I didn't get to dance enough," Susie said.

And Saeed snickered. "She make me tired, she dance so much."

"We were safe," Rick said. "We would have stayed longer, but we thought you might be worried."

There was no reason to suspect any danger between our house and Saeed's, but when I saw him about to go out into the night alone, I had an urgent impulse to invite him to spend the night. I knew I was contradicting myself already.

"Oh, yeah," Rick said, "we'll put our sleeping-bags on the living-room floor."

"It's O.K.?" Saeed said, looking at me, very pleased.

And Susie kissed me goodnight with unusual warmth.

There were a lot of other young people in and out of our house that summer—Nabeel, a boy of twenty who sometimes looked forty just after battles when he had seen things, maybe done things he didn't want to talk about; Adeeb, who had written a prize-winning song and was escaping to Paris; Saad, back from a lucrative job in Saudi Arabia, and his beautiful sister, Aziza; Nadia, whom I loved having around; and then Toufic, a skinny, bearded militiaman, who almost caused a fight between Susie and Saeed.

"Take care from him, because he's not nice," Saeed advised.

And Susie retorted, "Look who's telling me to be careful! Your girlfriend has the worst reputation in Lebanon."

"Who say that? Toufic? I think he want you riding in his car and not on my bike."

Rick was a calm and skillful arbitrator, and a moment later they laughed the incident away. Susie and Saeed and Rick remained a threesome that nobody else broke into and apparently nobody tried to break out of.

Once I saw them walking up the stairs, three abreast with their arms around one another, a tangle of suntans and sunburns, talking all at once in their crazy corrupt language, and it occurred to me to create a word like Arabish for what they were together, but I went on down the stairs and forgot, and then it was too late.

In August a weekend passed without our seeing Saeed. Susie fretted, and stood on the balcony and listened for his bike, and said things like, "I wonder where Saeed is?" And then on Monday afternoon she went to the swimming-pool alone and came back with a pinched look on her face. She said, "I guess the party's over. Allison is back." Her lips were twitching in the corners. At a moment like that there never is much a mother can say.

She sat down at the kitchen table and told me that Saeed was buzzing around Broummana with a girl on the back of his bike, a girl with long blond hair streaming out behind her. "I know I'm jealous," she said, "but it's more than that, too. She isn't good enough for him."

"What makes you say that?"

"Hunh! You should hear the guys in Broummana talk about her. And besides that, she doesn't even care about him. She treats him like dirt. I can't even believe some of the mean things she's done to him."

The inevitable had happened, I thought, but Susie would recover, and we could not blame Saeed too much since we had all somehow participated. But the summer grew stale very fast after that.

Sometimes Susie would get up in the morning thinking that surely he would come that day. She would get ready and wait, and she was reluctant to leave the house for anything, because she might miss him. In the afternoons she wouldn't even play records, because she was listening for the motorcycle. Finally, an hour before dinnertime, she would say to Rick, "Let's go *kizdiring*."

At first he took her, but later he started saying, "No. Because you're looking for Saeed, and when we find him you'll be more unhappy than you are now."

Her face grew dull and swollen, and there was nothing any of us could do to help. Maybe it was because she took it harder than I thought she would that I began to feel some resentment against Saeed, or maybe it was the discovery that all of us had been dropped.

Rick was packing and arranging tickets, because he was leaving a week ahead of Susie, and we were all walking around a little scared anyway, feeling that it was the end of a whole chapter in our lives. Just a couple of days before Rick had to leave, I went up to Broummana in the car to get some of his favorite Lebanese sweets for dinner, and I saw Saeed standing in front of a little restaurant with his hands in his pockets. I honked and then pulled over to the curb, and he crossed the street and took my hand, looking embarrassed.

I said, "Saeed, we miss you." I'm afraid there was as much accusation as friendliness in my voice.

His beautiful eyelashes were lying on his cheeks, and he said, "I know. I miss you, too. You become like my family, but I can't come and see you, because Allison, she don't let me."

"Why?"

"Because when she come back, everybody say to her, yeah, Saeed, he take another girl on his bike and you in London. She become very angry from me, and she say, it's them or me. You must to choose. And what can I do? Because I love her too much."

I said, "It's O.K., Saeed, for Roger and me, because we have lots of time, and maybe Allison will be our friend, too, someday, but it's very hard for the kids because they are leaving, and they need at least to say goodbye."

"Leaving? When are they leaving?"

"Rick goes on Thursday, and then Susie has just one more week."

"O.K.," he said. "I come and say goodbye."

"Can you come for dinner tomorrow night?"

"No, no, please. I can't, because it will be long time and Allison she will know. I come at five and a half."

"Five-thirty," I corrected him.

"Thanks. I come at five-thirty tomorrow for half hour."

He came, carrying the big helmet, combing his disorderly hair with his fingers, subdued, handsome in his bruised and crooked way.

Susie had made chocolate-chip cookies and washed her hair and made up her eyes, but she did a good job of acting lighthearted and relaxed. She teased Saeed and laughed a lot.

When he left, he said to Rick, "You are my brother," and kissed him on both cheeks. Then he looked around at the four of us and said, "You become my family, and I love you too much."

Finally he turned to Susie, his green eyes soft, and said, "Bye, Smarty-pants," and ran down the stairs quickly.

After Rick left, Roger and I spent as much time as we could with Susie and managed to get her talking about Cal Poly. I kept saying how exciting it was to start a new phase of life and meet lots of new people. Her daddy told her he was jealous of her and wished someone had made him study aeronautical engineering instead of history.

On the last full day she was at home she had the notion that Saeed would come, and as the afternoon faded into evening her face grew dark and heavy. At the moment she gave up, she said, "Last summer suave Samir. This summer Mr Universe." A little laugh and then, "That silly Rick. I miss him so much," and she began to cry.

When I woke her the next morning she stretched both arms into the air and shouted, "California, here I come!"

In the other room Roger said, "Uh oh. Lord help California."

At breakfast she said, "I'm flying today. Oh, Dad, just think. I'm going on the 747."

She was full of chatter. "Remember when I used to wish I were a bird? I really did. I used to watch a bird sitting on a tree limb or on a little bush and suddenly he would jump off and sail through the air, and I would think, oh, I wish I were a bird. I would just love it." And she laughed her old jolly laugh.

At the airport she hugged us, dry-eyed and eager to be going, and then halfway to the immigration gate, the heavy flight bag pulling down on her shoulder, she lifted her hand to wave with her ticket and passport, and her voice was full of a childish kind of pleading as she called, "Mom, tell Saeed to write to me."

I did tell him, a couple of weeks later when I happened to see him on the street, but he said he wasn't very good at writing.

Susie sent a letter to him enclosed in one of mine. She told me to read it to him if he had any trouble. I found him sitting on his motorcycle in front of Broummana High. He took the letter in his hand, stared at it and said, "For me?"

I gave him Susie's message, and he said, "Oh, no, I can read it," and shoved it into the pocket of his jacket, beaming.

But he never answered it.

Sometimes I felt I would miss Susie and Rick a little less if only Saeed would come.

At Cal Poly Susie got an A in physics and made the swim team. She wrote that a football player named Ted was a friend, "Maybe the best friend I ever had," and somebody named Jim had a brand new Kawasaki and often invited her to ride with him. Once she said that she still had Saeed's pictures on her tackboard, though she wasn't sure why.

In the spring there was a battle between two right-wing militia groups, and Toufic, the skinny militiaman, died. I was coming home from visiting his mother, and because of the shared sorrow, was full of relief and gratitude, thinking of my own children. If only I could see them for a few minutes, I thought, and suddenly noticed Saeed, standing idly against a storefront. When I stopped he walked over to the car but didn't even smile. He looked gray and tired and not at all like a little boy. I asked him if anything was wrong.

He said, "I have big trouble."

"Why don't you come and tell us about it?"

"Because I'm shamed," he said, "because you become my family and I don't come and see you for long time, and now I'm in trouble and need you and I'm shamed."

"Saeed, you are like our son. When a son is in trouble he should go home, even if he hasn't been there for a long time."

He came, and we listened to the jumbled pieces of a story about how Allison had kicked him out of her life.

"I hitted her," he said. "I know it's big sin hitting a woman. My father hitted my mother when he drunk, and I cry. And after he die, when I go see her, she tell me, don't drink alcohol and don't hit a woman, and 'til now I don't. But she hitted me first. I don't know a woman she hit a man. She make me, because she make me too much angry and I hitted her. Just I hitted her before I know. And I hurted her, and I don't like hurting her, because I love her too much, and now she won't let me say sorry.

"Every day I go to her house to say sorry and she don't let me come in. She don't speak with me. She lock the door, and when I knock the door she don't answer me.

"It's very hard when I make something bad and people they don't let me say sorry."

Just to help him, I tried to see Allison's viewpoint, and I said, "Give her a little time, Saeed. She'll feel different after she thinks it over."

"No," he said, "she won't. There's this rich man. Tall and good-looking and his family owns so much business. He has too much money and big house, and he want to marry her.

"For sure she marry him, because she's going around with him now, and she like money better than anything. She tell me once she never marry poor man, and I take eight hundred lira from the pharmacy, and she take two thousand from the school, and I know she never marry me. She want to sleep with me, but she never marry me.

"She's very bad girl. The first time I take her riding on my motorcycle, at the end she kiss me and ask me if I want to sleep with her. Of course, I want. I thought I should say no, and I thought she must be very bad girl, but I'm a man, and she's very beautiful, and I say yes. And she complicated me too much, because I think that I'm making big sin, and I can't stop. Only now she don't let me in."

Sometimes he would break off the story, saying, "I hate her, and I never want to see her again."

Though I was finding out why Allison wasn't "good enough for Saeed," she was actually growing unexpectedly in my mind, redeemed somehow by his loving her so much.

He would drink a little tea, the cup trembling in his hands, and start over.

"She's embarrassed about me. She want me living with her, but when she go to the school for parties and programs she don't let me go with her. Because I'm not educated. All the people there they are teachers, and they speak like professors, and she's embarrassed about me, because I don't speak very well English.

"And you know me, sometime I act like little boy. I don't know why, just something come to my mind and I say it or do it, and she's embarrassed about me.

"And what can I do? I am thirty years almost. I tell everybody I'm twenty-five, but I'm thirty almost, and I don't know to do anything but ride the motorcycle and take the medicine to the people. And what's my life here? Maybe in some other country I learn something new and have good work, but in Lubnan I can do nothing.

"She like to have money and beautiful things. She want to buy house in Lubnan. Every month I give her all my money. If I don't give her money she make me go away. My mother she say she's bad woman and does things for money." He hit his head with his fist and groaned, "Why I love her so much?"

We listened until we were almost as exhausted as Saeed. And finally he said, "Pray for me, and maybe my God will help me."

Fearful things happened in Lebanon the next few days; the university suspended classes temporarily, and we had too much time to think and talk. Roger thought it was providential for Saeed that he had been jilted, and I discovered that I understood Allison surprisingly well. It was one thing for a girl to ride on a motorcycle, or to be in love, with a young man as warm and attractive as Saeed, but it was another thing for an educated young woman to have a husband who couldn't hold a decent job or speak any language correctly. Her feelings must be as contradictory as his, I decided.

And then he came again, kissing me at the door and saying, "You become like my mother." He said that God had helped him, and he was going to forget about Allison and never see her again. "She's very bad girl, and she spoil my life."

He was upset, however, about something else that had happened since we saw him. While in the neighborhood his mother lived in he had dropped by the headquarters of a right-wing militia group to say hello to a friend of his, and while he was there, a group of militiamen dragged in a young Muslim whom they had caught on the street in their community.

"He was just a boy," Saeed said, "maybe fifteen, and they were screaming, he's Muslim, what for is he here in our neighborhood? They wanted to kill him, and I said, no, he is a boy. Look, he has no weapon. What can he do to anybody? Let him go. And the boy he was crying, because he was scared from what they would do to him. And I said, give me him, and I take him on the motorbike to his house.

"So one of them he push the boy against the wall and he say, Saeed is your friend, not ours, and he will take you to your home, and then he just shoot him. Two times he shoot him."

Saeed turned pale and looked a little sick.

"Then they tell me, take him, he is yours. But, of course, I can't. If I go across the Green Line with a dead Muslim on my bike, they are going to kill me over there."

I felt so stunned I kept staring at Saeed's face, trying to see all the ways he had been injured by this brutality, and he turned those wonderful green eyes away to hide his emotion. Roger got up and squeezed some orange juice and popped some popcorn. "We never have any chocolate-chip cookies," he said, "since Susie left."

Saeed smiled faintly into his juice and said, "How is she?"

"Great!" Roger said. "She's very happy there."

"And Rick?"

I read a few lines from Rick's last letter. "I am playing my new Fairouz record while I write this. Her voice is beautiful like Lebanon, and it makes me a little homesick."

Saeed said, "Let him stay there. It's better."

"Yes," I agreed. "It's better."

"I want to go somewhere," he said, "because I'm tired from this war and tired from my life, and I must to become somebody."

We tried to talk about his options, but there did not seem to be any. Finally he said, "If Lebanese man marry American girl, can he get visa and go to America?"

I said, "Yes."

"For sure?"

"For sure."

"But," Roger said, "you can't marry a girl just to get a visa."

"Oh, no," he said, "but I'm thinking if I like American girl and she like me, it's good, and if I marry any girl, I will live with her and I will be good with her."

Another time I was writing to Susie, sitting at the dining-room table. Roger was across the table trying to balance his checkbook, and Saeed sat between us. He was getting more relaxed all the time and that night the conversation was lighter, and I kept on writing. He said, "Are you writing letters?"

"Yes, to Susie."

"Tell her *salam* from Saeed." Then he said, "No, I will write and send the letter with yours."

I gave him paper and a pen, and he said, "How you write Dear Smarty-pants?"

After he had written that he said, "She can read it, can't she, if I write Arabic?"

I wasn't too happy about sending her a letter she had ached for so long and then forgotten about, but I did. And when a week had gone by he started asking every day about an answer. Finally, we received a letter which said, "I enjoyed Saeed's note. Tell him I will write as soon as I get time."

According to Susie she got four letters altogether. She wrote that the first one was friendly, reminding her of the summer's fun. The second was affectionate and came before she answered the first one. The third was "mushy." These reports were odd, coming from Susie, because they were given without comment or reaction.

"I'm scared," I told Roger.

"Why?"

"Because I know how much he loves Allison."

"Doesn't Susie know that, too?"

"I guess so. But still... if he asks her to marry him..." I didn't know how to finish the sentence.

"Don't worry," Roger said. "Susie has her head on straight."

I said, "I don't worry about her head."

She called very early one Sunday morning to tell us that she had a neat job for the summer, something about running a computer at an air-force base in southern California. "I'm so excited," she said. "I can't wait to see those airplanes!"

Her dad said, "Big deal, you can hear them from inside your office."

"Don't kid yourself," she said. "I'm gonna talk myself onto some airplanes."

"Susie," he said, "they won't let you fly."

"Just you wait," she told him. "Mom, I've got to hang up while I can still pay for this, but I need to ask you about Saeed. I have another letter from him. Now he's asked me to marry him. And Mom, I'm just wondering... well, I mean... what is his problem?"

When we hung up I felt so relieved I wanted to laugh, except I was sad, because what was going to happen to Saeed?

He stayed away for several weeks, and when he came again it was to talk about Allison. She had broken the long silence by leaving a note at the pharmacy asking him to come. "She want me to forget about what happen and marry her," he said. "She is buying apartment near school. It will be her apartment, by herself, but only I live in it with her. She say her money hers, and my money mine. She say when she go to London one month in summer I not go with her. I want to ask you, is this marriage?"

I didn't think the answer really mattered, so I didn't say anything.

Roger said, "Maybe it's not the best kind."

Saeed said, "I know she will be embarrassed from me and make me stay in the house when she go to the school, but if I only live with her, *ma'leish*, I don't care. Only I hope she treat me like big man and not like little boy."

In the middle of explaining it all, he said, "I ask Susie to marry me, but she say no. I think if I ask her last summer she say yes, but I miss my chance."

I didn't know what to say. I remembered Susie and Rick and Saeed chattering in Arabish, coming up the stairs laughing, with their arms around each other. It seemed possible that we had all missed some kind of a chance.

He was looking at me, and finally I said, "I know," and then he went back to talking about Allison.

"I'm scared," he said, "because maybe she have another boyfriend in London, and the man at the British Consul he tell me I can't take visa just because I marry British girl. If she want to leave me forever someday, she can go to London, and I can't do anything.

"What do you think?" he finished.

I said, "I think I feel scared, too."

"But what can I do? My life has no other place to go."

In early September Susie called again because she was so "jazzed" about all the wonderful things that were happening to her and just had to tell us. Suddenly she had been assigned to work with a test pilot, and her tasks included being present for all his briefings and doing his paperwork.

"Are you listening, Dad?" Her words tumbled all over each other as she told us that she had been in the air twice. Once she handled the controls of the F-135 for a few minutes, and the second time she flew the boom to refuel another plane.

Her dad said, "O.K., Smarty-pants. You win."

When I told her that Saeed had married Allison, there was a sudden silence in California. I waited. Finally she said, "Mom, I hope she's going to be good to him," and it almost seemed that she was crying.

The war is always worse in summer, so we don't let Rick and Susie come. Sometimes in the late afternoons I catch myself listening for the sound of a certain motorcycle, but Saeed doesn't come either. I'm not sure what that means. The mountains are the same fragile lavender at sundown, and Roger and I make a lot of shish kabob on the balcony.

The Crucifier

On his way to mass on Sunday morning Waleed already knew that he was in trouble. For months now a subtle danger had been following him, creeping up around him like a fog, penetrating his veins like a wicked spirit. He knew how to face an attacking army and how to listen for unfriendly footsteps, but this threat was silent and unassailable, like an illness. Yes, maybe he was sick. But Waleed strolled through the village in his usual Sunday-morning manner— smiling, greeting people, deliberately aware of his handsome self in his immaculate navy-blue suit and bright tie, determinedly conscious of his dutiful self, a man who had been wounded for his country— all the while avoiding the memory of what had happened last night.

The road he walked along passed the bottom steps of the houses on the up side of the hill and looked down on the flat roofs of those on the other side. From these roofs and steps, from balconies and fields, the neighbors spoke or waved to him as he passed. Aunt Siham, everybody's aunt because she was so old, sitting on her haunches in a field of wild greens, looked up from her work and said, "Good morning, good-looking."

And he answered, "Good morning, Aunt. Beautiful day, isn't it?"

Abu Elias, with a sour face, grunted as he jerked the flat tire off his dusty jalopy, and said, "How are you, Waleed?" The smell of rubber and grease floated up around him.

"God give you strength, Abu Elias. Fine, thank you."

The respectful voices of these neighbors comforted him. They knew him, and he was sure that they saw him as he wanted to see himself, like the sweet-faced young man on the poster which hung for months on the windows and walls of the town, a soldier kneeling in church, slender and worshipful, as opposed to the vicious Druze, waving his curved sword on the other side of the poster. The people of the town owed their safety to him and the others who had fought to defend them. They knew; they were grateful.

As he thought this, Waleed stroked his squarish, freshly shaved chin, because he enjoyed the clean feel of it, and because he wondered. A few weeks ago he had removed the beard, which was a badge worn by militiamen. He did not understand this himself. He liked his beard, and yet, needled by his own doubts, his uneasiness, he had arranged a new face to look at in the mirror.

All he had ever wanted, and he thought of it often, was respect—from himself and others. For this a man did his duty on the battlefield, took care of his parents, and followed the practices of his religion. In all arenas he had excelled; he had done a little more than necessary. He had fought with valor, even recklessness. He was a respectful and obedient son. And not only did he go to confession and communion weekly, but he read a few verses of scripture each day. Most people did not, he knew. Yesterday morning he read just a paragraph about the crucifixion from one of the Gospels. But when he remembered, walking through the village in the sunshine, a shadow fell across his heart, and he stopped smiling, was not able anymore to fake this smile. He had not finished reading the story. Reflexively, as one might dodge a blow, he had quit in the middle of a sentence and flipped the pages.

He never read with any plan, believing in the magic of what fell under his eye each day. What had fallen under his eye next on that Saturday was, "Vengeance is mine, I will repay, says the Lord." And Waleed closed the book, feeling betrayed. Twice in five minutes the magic had turned malevolent. Long after he ate his breakfast the words he had read still pricked and stung.

On the way to church, his shoes shiny against the blacktop road, spring flowers, yellow and red and violet, popping their heads up between the rocks, children in their Sunday clothes spilling down the long stairways from their houses up the hill, Waleed noticed that Bulous' gigantic prickly-pear cactus was putting out little green knobs which would be yellow fruit by the end of summer, and he thought that reading the Bible was sometimes like eating the juicy, sweet meat of the prickly pear. The words made him feel satisfied and fortunate. And other times reading it was like clasping the thorny, unpeeled fruit in his naked hand. It made him cry out with pain and be sorry he had done it.

He was ready to acknowledge (though only to himself) that the crucifixion was not a story one wanted to read. He could not read it, because when he did, he saw things. They flashed into his head so quickly that he was horrified before he could stop them. He saw the swift, panting struggle, a hand being held against the wood, fingers being forced open, a coarse, callused hand with dirt under the nails, clenching and twisting, trying to avoid the point of the nail. He heard laughter. He felt the softness of flesh giving way under the impact of steel (this softness surprised him) and the hardness of wood under the hand. He heard screams.

This vision had haunted him for more than a year. It invaded his dreams, and he woke in the darkness, sweating, with his heart pounding. Sometimes it waited for him in church, so that his image of himself, the slender youth with a pure face, kneeling before a row of candles, was replaced by the image of a murderer, wiping sweat from his face, sitting on his hands to conceal their trembling. And then he would discover that he really was wiping his face and then sitting on his uncontrollable hands.

But on Saturday afternoon he had chased this problem and all the bad pictures out of his mind, because Waleed did not usually give any space in his head to a worry or a doubt or a thorn that wouldn't come out yet. He took his basketball to the clubhouse and started trying to round up some fun. There weren't enough people for a regular game, but he knew he had to keep moving, so he organized two-on-two and finally one-on-one competitions and kept himself dribbling and pivoting and shooting and rebounding all afternoon. Though he had lost part of the muscle on his thigh, his leg was almost as strong as before he had been injured. It hardly hurt anymore. He had exercised it several times a day, beginning with prescribed movements under hot water, as soon as the doctor took the stitches out, when it was stiff and sore.

He played until nearly dark, then he came home, "smelling like a horse," his mother said, showered and shaved, put on perfume and a pretty shirt and took his girl dancing. Afterwards they sat in his car and kissed and touched. He had planned every move, so that one thing would lead to another and there would be no stopping place.

And suddenly, unexplainably, it had gone wrong, after she was so cooperative and sweet and he had started to feel safe from gory imaginations. He did not yet understand what had happened. She had begun to pant and to whisper, "No, no, no," not telling him to stop but telling herself that it was too late to stop. She was writhing in eagerness, but still a little scared, so he held her more fiercely and pushed her against the seat of the car and suddenly, irrationally, he remembered the smell of blood, felt nauseated, and released her. For a moment she struggled, surprised and lost, against the swift current in which he had abandoned her.

On the way to church, under the shade of a row of tall pine trees, he burned with the humiliation of this impotence, this weakness, of taking her to her home in Ashrafiyeh and saying goodnight and having no words with which to rescue the evening and make a bridge to next time. And then he realized that he was walking so slowly, because he dreaded the mass. The whole thing was hideous with its references to death and blood and flesh. And, of course, he could not go in and participate unless he first confessed his sins. And he had walked almost to the church without working out what he ought to say.

He supposed that he would have to say something about last night. He could not tell the whole truth, of course. A priest would not reveal what he heard at confession, but he would remember and he would use it. If he knew everything, he would have a look of contempt on his face when Waleed met him on the street. He would put some kind of obstacle in the way, if one day Waleed wanted to marry another girl, not that one. It would take a lot of money to move the obstacle.

But maybe this worry was premature, when he did not even know how to get another evening with Jumana. Maybe she felt hurt this morning. Or angry. He knew so little about what was inside her pretty head, not even how much she really liked him. Then he wondered if she would go to church this morning. Would she talk about him in the confession box? These questions moved and frightened him. Maybe the priest would advise her to avoid him and to keep herself pure like the Virgin Mother. Would she take such advice seriously?

For sure he could not confess anything about what had happened last year over in the Chouf. He could not even think about it, much less talk, but until now he had had a strategy for evasion, had driven its images away by filling his mind with beautiful thoughts about girls, and now maybe he had lost his surest refuge. Even at this moment the crucifixion was coming back to him again. The images pushed in between him and the face of old man Maadi, who was trying to decide whether to get in the confession line or not.

What an obscene thing was the death of Jesus, especially because it was so useless. Maybe some people read the Bible and saw a pretty picture of three crosses, evenly spaced, silhouetted against the sky, with nice, mannerly people (even the criminals were mild and accepting fellows) hanging there quietly. But whenever Waleed tried to visualize this picture-postcard crucifixion, it tipped and smeared and jumbled. There was blood on the sky, like in a sloppy painting, and bodies scattered around on the ground, and Jesus was jerking his shoulder to try to tear his hand loose. He had thought several times that he should tell the priest about this, that he should admit that coming to church was getting harder and harder because he did not want to be reminded of this story. In fact, he should challenge the church's claim that this death was necessary and should be reviewed every Sunday. But something always stopped him. He had never told the priest anything from deep down, anything that really mattered.

It was better to say something about his sexual temptations. No doubt the father-confessor was a man underneath those skirts. He would not be shocked, at least as long as he did not know the whole of it, the things Waleed had done, and last night had not been able to do.

The woman who was ahead of him did not stay long, Mr Maadi had disappeared, and suddenly it was his turn, though he had not yet decided what to say. He pushed aside the curtain, which was red and dusty, the same as it had been the first time he went to confession when he was only eight. Inside the dim little cubicle he knelt, facing the latticed window. He saw the vague, shadowy shape of a man's face on the other side and heard someone say, "Yes, son. What is it?"

The dimness and the moldy smell tended to make Waleed feel dirty and to think his darkest thoughts, but when he spoke he was surprised to hear a quiver in his voice.

"Last night," he whispered. Then he cleared his throat to get rid of the shaky sound and said, "Sorry, Father, my throat is not feeling well."

"*Salamtak*," the priest said.

After the blessing on his health, Waleed tried again, aware in some remote corner of his mind that he had already lied. He said, "Last night I was with this girl."

He hesitated, thinking he must be very quiet, because he could feel the others waiting just beyond the curtain, and the priest said, "Yes?" expectantly.

"I mean I took her dancing."

"Yes." A yes that meant only, "I'm listening."

"Well, she was very beautiful and very... well, tempting in my arms, and I had very bad ideas."

"Ideas. Only ideas?"

"Well, you see, I felt frustrated and when I went home I kept thinking bad thoughts, and I could not sleep."

"Lascivious thoughts are not desirable, son. It is not wise to hold them in the mind and enjoy them, but do not confuse temptation with sin. Is there anything else?"

"Yes," he said, "I crucified a man."

He did not mean to say it. He didn't know where the words came from, just suddenly they were already said. When he realized this, the blood surged through his veins as cold as the river, and the silence on the other side of the window filled him with alarm. It was like the time he dropped a hand grenade inside the militia headquarters. The men had all been rubbing their guns or dialing the phone or laughing about the dunce who shot himself in the foot, and when the grenade fell it clattered on the tile floor, and suddenly they were all stiff, even their words frozen in the air. Then they heard the silence and someone saw the pin in the grenade, and they all knew they were alive. But before anybody else could move or speak, the officer slapped him.

He waited in front of the little window to be slapped, or at least to know that the pin was in and there would be no explosion.

Finally, the priest said, "Last night?"

"Oh, no, a long time ago."

"Does this have anything to do with the girl?"

"No, no. I have only known the girl a few months. This happened before."

"When?"

"During the Battle of the Chouf."

Again the priest was silent for a long time. "During the battle you did it?"

"Yes, Father." He shifted his knees, because the board under them was beginning to be very hard.

"Why?"

"I don't know."

"There were others with you?"

He hesitated. Confession was only for oneself. "Yes," he said finally, "there were others."

And again the priest said, "Why?"

"I don't know."

"Did you talk about it together and plan it?"

"No. Just we began to do it. I mean, one thing led to another, and after we started there was no way to stop." Even as he spoke he remembered fear and wild anger and then euphoria, a wonderful feeling of freedom and invincibility. They had been caught up by a mysterious force, a high they did not understand.

"Who was this man?"

"An enemy. A Druze."

Once more there was silence in the dimness behind the window. Waleed began to panic again, like maybe the pin was not in the grenade. He was trembling deep inside.

"You didn't know him at all?"

"No." He did not mean for the word to come out so quickly, as though he needed to hurry the conversation.

"Had he done anything to you?"

"He resisted our advance." Whether they were advancing or retreating, he was unsure now, but it didn't matter. "He had a gun and shot at us from a window. Then we went in and found him."

"Was he alone?"

"No. He had... a woman and a bunch of crying kids." He was starting to sweat and shifted his knees once more. One did not expect to be interrogated during confession.

"What happened to them?"

"He yelled at them to run, and we let them run." This was not exactly true, but the truth was so hard to explain, and he had to get this over with.

"And then?"

"We nailed him to a door."

After a long wait, during which Waleed could hear himself breathing, the priest said, "They complained of atrocities. I spoke on television and gave my word that there were no atrocities."

"I know, Father. You are a man who knows his duty."

"A day of reprisals could come."

Vengeance. Waleed had thought of that. They would want vengeance. He said, "I know; that's why you spoke."

"Son, this is a very grave matter, and you must do some act of penance. I order you to go to the statue of the Virgin, crawl on your knees up to her feet and say twenty Hail Marys. She will understand. She knows our history better than we do. Leave an offering there for the poor. Be generous. I will pray for you now."

While the priest prayed for him in the dark behind the lattice, Waleed recited in a whisper the memorized words of contrition, feeling short of breath, aware of a small, twisting pain in his stomach.

"Now go in to the communion," the priest told him. "God's grace will come to you in the sacred bread and wine."

"Thank you, Father."

The church was dark and cool, and Waleed, surrounded by his own darkness, was barely aware of the blur of color and movement in the pews, the low hum of voices, the whine of the organ, the flicker of candles. He made the sign of the cross, stumbled into a pew and sat down. A priest was chanting the scripture in a nasal tone, an unpleasant sound which resonated with the buzz in his head. The pain in his stomach grew worse.

Dropping onto the kneeling board in front of him, he buried his head in his arms and saw the man's face for the millionth time, saw him so startled, like he couldn't believe something that bad could happen to him. The room was littered with bodies and puddles of blood, though some of the children did escape. The faces of the panicked kids flashed before him, and that begging gesture of the little one, who reached for his father.

If only those scraps of lumber and the tools had not been there. One of the militiamen picked up the hammer and the can of nails and had an idea. "Brilliant!" another said.

That was a clumsy business, nailing him to the door. First they tried to do it with the door in place, opened against the wall. And then someone said, "That won't work, stupid." And after they took the door off its hinges and threw the man down on it, he remembered. While driving the first nail he remembered seeing a film of the crucifixion of Jesus. They had nailed him to the cross on the ground and then picked it up and dropped it into a hole.

Because the door was too narrow, they had to bend the man's arms and put his hands just above his head. They had to pull up his knees to get the soles of his feet flat against the door, and the Druze fought while they were doing it. He kicked so much, it was like he had six legs. Some of the men were yelling, "Crucify him! Crucify him!"

along with a lot of obscenities, and the more he fought the more they said it. It took everybody to hold his feet, and then they discovered that the fool had torn one of his hands loose. They pushed it down again, making the head of the nail come through the back of his hand. This was a messy maneuver that got blood on several people. The Druze tossed his head around and strained all the muscles in his face, closing his eyes tight and trying to keep his mouth shut against a cry of pain. Then Waleed, holding the man's wrist, had hammered the nail sideways and bent the head. While he was leaning over to strike the nail, the smell of the man's blood rose into Waleed's nose and stuck to his tongue. Suddenly his head reeled, and he feared he would be sick. He was kneeling over the man, holding him by the wrist and trying not to faint.

In the car he had taken Jumana's wrists, wrists so slender and feminine that in other moments they made his fingers tingle. When he pinned them down on either side of her face, it happened. There was this eager movement of her body, and then she closed her eyes, and a door opened in himself, letting images of the crucifixion jump out. He had not noticed before that desire was a lot like panic and pleasure so much like pain. The same faint feeling that had overcome him in the Chouf came back, and his whole body went limp.

From the sounds around him Waleed knew that people were going one by one to the altar to receive the holy bread. The taste of blood lingered in his mouth and the dread of going forward made his limbs heavy, but surely he would receive grace from eating the bread and waiting while the priest drank the wine for him. They would turn into the body and blood of Christ and save him somehow. And he desperately needed this.

It was his turn, and he went heavily as in a nightmare, his legs undependable, the room reeling, the ghostly face of Christ contorting as the nail went through his palm with a slight, rubbery resistance. He struggled, ripped his right hand loose. Stronger hands put it back, and a cry tore out of his throat. People were laughing and crying and yelling, "Crucify him!"

Confession was supposed to be good for the soul, but it had not been good. A second time in this one life, he had tripped with the grenade in his hand. Pain twisted in his gut, and the terrifying shadow of nausea crept through his body.

The young priest waited for him, severe and handsome in a white robe, with a gold-stitched surplice and a thick cross on his chest. A boy stood beside him, a beautiful boy, holding the plate to put under Waleed's chin, so no crumb of the body of Christ could fall to the floor. For a moment Waleed could see only this boy, as though a light fell upon him, leaving everything else in darkness. The child's face held the purity of one who believes in what he is doing and his eyes shone with a kind of love.

A memory struck Waleed, leaving him stunned and alert, with his face burning. Once, standing beside the priest, holding up the plate to protect the sacrament, he had been such a boy. He had stood right here in this church, pure and honest. His sense of loss mingled with the pungency of the incense around the altar and the smell of melting wax, as the priest held the bread, a mere flake, in one hand, extending it toward him. "This is the lamb of God, that takes away the sin of the world."

He opened his mouth and felt the priest's fingers touch his tongue for an instant, and then he discovered that he could not swallow. He stumbled back to his seat, holding his lips closed, thankful to have the bench safely under him, turning his face away from a woman who entered the pew, tying a scarf under her fat chin. The wafer soured on his tongue and saliva gushed behind his lips, before finally he swallowed.

The priest was holding the silver chalice, lifting it high, chanting the ancient words of the mass. Then he lowered the cup, and Waleed heard clearly, "This is my blood which was shed for you." As he tipped it to his lips, Waleed imagined the blood running, thick and warm, into his own mouth and knew that he must escape.

Noisily, like a frightened horse, he bolted, running up the aisle, past the blur in the pews and a group of little girls in white dresses outside the door, and not knowing where he was going, holding one hand over his mouth, he turned the corner of the building and plunged headlong into the small forest below the church. There he hid behind a tree and vomited. He vomited the body of Christ, along with the *mana'ooshy* he had eaten for breakfast. He stood up once, then bent and retched again. Still heaving, the heaves hurting, he wondered what it meant to have one's stomach refuse the sacrament. The thought made his skin cold and sweaty. Had anyone ever before in the history of Christianity thrown up the communion bread? Was this a sign that God had rejected him?

Staggering farther down the hill, he fell on his face in the pine needles. He should feel better now that he had vomited, but instead he was sick all over. His body turned suddenly hot although his teeth were chattering. Even the smell of the needles, crushed by his elbows, was sickening. He rose to his knees, then doubled over and leaned on his forearms, holding his head in his hands. After a while, when a little stone began to cut his knee, he sat up and propped against a tree, feeling the bark rough through his coat. His heart was pounding fearfully, more than during a time-out at a basketball game, more than in the heat of battle. He tried to calm himself by breathing evenly.

Cautiously, he opened his eyes and squinted into the light under the tree limbs, across the tops of the snobars down the hill. The roof of the forest sloped steeply into the canyon, where the little river ran cold and clear. On the other side, the towns of the Chouf basked in the morning sun, the yellow and brown and red and green colors of stone and roof tile and gardens, all a little blurred by a light spring haze. In a village out of sight, on the other slope of the mountain, he had left a man nailed to the door, blood oozing from his hands and feet, the door tipped slightly backward against the wall. The man's face, raging with anger and pain, had grown frantic, seeing they would leave him, and he began to gasp and fainted. While they were picking up their guns and pissing on the bodies on the floor, he came around again and said something. Waleed heard the word "remember."

"He's going to remember this," he told the others. They laughed.

"Of course," someone said. "He is Druze. The instant he dies, he will be born." Laughter. "His new mother is in labor right now." For a while laughter had blotted out the sound of screaming echoing in his head.

The trees and rocks and cliffs along the edges of the canyon marked its twisting path until it disappeared into the misty crevices between the hills. There the earth rose and spread out at the same time, becoming the broad hovering mountain. When he was a child he thought that God lived there and watched all the world from the top of Sunnin. The world to him, then and now, was these forests and terraces, these tumbled mountains with the canyon between, the singing springtime river, watched over by the great mountain and God. Except lately it seemed that the mountain was vacant. Nobody there.

He could not recall just when God had left, or exactly when his life had taken a puzzling, downhill turn. Maybe God had deserted him in anger. But, even if he knew this, Waleed could not go back and change anything. The crucifixion was already part of the story of his life, along with the lost battles, the foolish accidents, and Jumana.

He would obey the priest. He would go more than once. He would say more than twenty Hail Marys. He would give to the poor, even to the Druze poor. But it was not possible ever to escape the images of that day.

They did all those same things to Jesus, and stripped him naked too and spit on him. From the cross he looked up toward heaven and said, "Father, forgive them." That was disgusting. Waleed had always wanted to say so, to confront some priest, to challenge God on this point. Suppose that dirty Druze had stopped struggling and said, "I forgive you." Or looked up at the ceiling and prayed for them. How they would have laughed at him! Forgiveness was stupid. It had always made Waleed angry. How could he? And now Waleed beat his fist on the root of the tree and shouted, "How could you? Why? Why should you?"

His words flew across the canyon and came back in fragments, and then the earth was quiet. The trees stood still. No needle fell, no donkey brayed. Only the silly cicadas, wherever they were, filled the air with "zzzzzzzz." It was a noise akin to silence. It could drive one crazy, or it could go totally unnoticed. He tried not to notice. He had shouted at God. He felt stronger now. Let God answer, if he wanted.

Slowly he relaxed. The sun grew warm. The light made him want to shut his eyes. A fuzziness overcame him, and he thought that he would sleep just a moment. In his sleep someone sat beside him and whispered in his ear. Waleed could not see the person, but he felt breath on his face and heard a quiet voice. The voice said, "You are despicable."

Immediately he knew that the words were true and that the voice was God's. He tried to call God's name but could not make a sound.

Then the voice said, "You crucified me."

Waleed struggled to speak, was not sure he did. "No. Not me. I mean, he was your enemy."

"You haven't understood anything."

Waleed was surprised by this reply and did not know what it meant.

God said, "Did I appoint you to punish my enemies?"

"No. I guess not," he answered, finding a voice at last.

"Or did I die for my enemies?"

Waleed found himself reluctant to admit this.

"Am I a partial God?"

"No. You died for the world."

"Why did you do it?"

Waleed tried to think of excuses. Maybe the history, buried deep in their genes, had something to do with it. Maybe war was a drug that had messed up their heads. But with the breath of God warm on his ear, these thoughts seemed silly.

"I don't know," he whispered.

"Then neither will I tell you why I forgave them. I am God. I always act like God, so I have nothing to explain."

Waleed felt bolder then and let his voice rise again. "Well, let me tell you, God. I wouldn't. If I were the one nailed to a piece of wood, or even my brother or my father or my comrade in battle, I would hate the man with the hammer and nails forever. With all my strength, I would hate him."

"Yes. That was implied in the words you shouted."

"I wanted to say them for years."

"You don't like my way?"

Suddenly Waleed woke, his head falling forward, his mind reaching back for the dream, a strange, incomplete dream. Behind him on the road beyond the church, a car puttered past, missing on one cylinder. A dog was barking. He was afraid. Something had changed while he slept. Someone had joined him in the forest. He was not alone. He looked around and saw no one. Certain that someone was watching him, he sat rigid, startled. The back of his neck prickled, but when he turned again there was still nobody.

"God?" he said, trembling, forming the word but not making a sound.

"You don't like my way?" God had said.

Waleed laid a hand on his chest, where he suddenly felt a shortness of breath. Was God saying that he had no right to be called a Christian?

Audibly he said, "I... I just can't beg for forgiveness. O.K.?" And then, as clearly as if God had answered, he understood why. Because then he might have to sympathize with beggars. With shirkers. With cowards. With pagans. With...

He felt startled and caught. He had been wrong about so many things. But had God really come to him? And spoken? In his dream? In this forest? He got up, wandered around, kicking at twigs and last year's pine cones, trying to think. This was implausible. He would walk away, go home. This would all seem silly once he was in the house, eating lunch. He would have a glass of arak and take a nap.

But when he turned and took a step, he stumbled over a mere twig and stopped to shake it off his shoe. The presence in the forest seemed to close in on him, solid and vibrant and more stubborn than he. Where he walked, it followed. Again he started up the path toward home but realized just then that falling asleep was dangerous. He might have another nightmare or another conversation with God. When he woke he would remember that he was a murderer and could not love a girl anymore. Could it have been God shadowing him all these months? The thought stopped his feet. And his breath. He could see the road snaking through the snobars, the road which he had walked with dread toward the church. The screech of the cicadas pierced his head. He picked up a stone and hurled it against a tree. Suddenly there was silence.

He glanced up at Sunnin, feeling a pang of longing for the god who had lived up there on the mountain and never interfered in his life. Would he ever have peace again? The other one died, he thought, and I, the crucifier, remain alive, hanging from my torn hands. He looked at his hands, clenched them and covered his eyes with his fists.

"God!" he cried out. The word hung on the silence for a moment, and then he said, "Are you going to keep following me?"

Yes. Otherwise you will be alone.

Out of the silence this came to him clearly, and he knew it was true. He stood there, with his knuckles against his eyeballs, not knowing whether he had fallen finally into hope or despair. "Help me," he said, his voice strangled. "God help me."

When he opened his eyes, he saw the atmosphere radiant. Sunshine filled the forest. It flashed from a million needles. It lighted the green moss on tree trunks. It threw a golden circle around a patch of red poppies and, under the trees, touched lightly the pale, bent heads of cyclamen. The air seemed charged with energy, with something about to happen. His knees felt weak. Surely this was a holy place, or a holy moment. He was surrounded, not by sunshine and flowers, but by cleanness and goodness, or maybe a crowd of good friends. His heart leaped and then grew very still, and he lived a while without breathing or thinking. Finally, he unclenched his fists, dropped his head on his chest and whispered, "Me, too, God. Forgive me."

For an instant his face burned with shame; then the feeling passed, and he was only surprised, that he had done it, that he was standing there, relieved, not knowing himself anymore, and not knowing how to feel or what to expect next. How, he wondered, was he supposed to know, when he asked forgiveness, that he had been heard and forgiven, or not?

68

While he waited, a great calmness encircled him. Like friendly hands it touched his hair and his skin. Then a certainty came up from inside of him, came in an irresistible rush like a wave of the ocean. All his torments were being lifted on this wave, lifted like bits of trash and borne away. The scarred battlefield in the middle of his self was bathed in warm liquid. God had heard him. He was sure. God had come down from Sunnin and pursued him and answered his prayer. The surprise of it made tears spring to his eyes. Still weeping, he began to laugh a little, tentatively, the way people do sometimes after battles, discovering that they are alive. He walked around, lifting his arms in elation, laughing and wiping tears. He was astonished to find himself so happy. When had he ever been so happy?

Without deciding to go, he was loping down the long hill toward home, the pine trees brilliant, the world alive with colors and voices and lovely shapes and smells, when a thought occurred to him. If Jesus had not died, if those ignoramuses who didn't know what they were doing had not killed Jesus, there would have been no way out for him, Waleed. He couldn't have said, Me too.

Thinking this, he staggered and hesitated. Was not this truth too heavy to walk down the road with? And immediately he began to suspect that everything showed on his body. Was he limping, like after his injury, like Jacob after he wrestled with an angel? Maybe his face was shining, like Moses' did, coming down from Sinai. Did he look like someone who had been on a long journey? He started brushing the pine needles off his coat and his tie and his knees and the seat of his trousers. His mother would not say, "You are late for lunch." She would say, "We have missed you," and search his face with her eyes. He would not know how to answer. Were there words for what had happened to him? And finally he realized that he had no idea how one lived after meeting with God and being forgiven, or what other incredible events could happen in this life.

Human Battles

A man began to shout in the street just in front of the house of Abu Elias. What we, the nearest neighbors, heard him say was, "Women should not be like this." No doubt it was this remark, more than the anger in his voice, that made our whole end of the village become attentive. People turned on their balconies, a bare-chested boy walking with an ice-cream bar paused to eavesdrop, and Malcolm and I left our Boggle game to look out the window.

It was Sunday afternoon, and in spite of war and suspense, some Sunday afternoons are just the way Lebanese Sunday afternoons are supposed to be. People drive out of the city to visit friends in the village. Grown offspring come home to their parents, bringing grandchildren. The children strip the fruit trees. Gambling games break out between the coffee cups. Church bells ring, and decorated cars take brides to the church, honking, honking.

In the midst of all this normal clatter, the man began to shout. "Women should not be like this!" he said. So we looked out the window just as a small head popped out of a fig tree and the boy with the ice-cream bar paused. We saw that the man was Haroun, Abu Elias' son-in-law. He was a big, burly man, with a bristly mustache, and at the moment his face was twisted by a helpless fury. He was looking up at his father-in-law's house shouting, his voice like a dog's bark, his sentences thrown like rocks.

"In all the world," he yelled, "women are not like this. You are unreasonable. You are worthless. You are trash." With each statement he threw out his arms in the direction of the house, extending them palms up in a gesture not so much like fighting as like appealing for help.

Abu Elias' house stands on the hillside above the road, and most of what is visible to a person standing below it is the grapevine which shades the patio at the entrance. The clutter of this patio is merely suggested by the row of scraggly flowers planted in rusty tin cans, the iron spring protruding from the back of an old couch and the refrigerator by the front door.

Haroun shouted and gestured toward this clutter, for there was no one on the patio, but when a high-pitched stream of words came back, he did not appear to hear. He leaned to take the hand of his child. I had not noticed the little boy before. He was looking up toward the house, with the baffled concern of one too young to understand why grown-ups shout. He was a dark, handsome boy, handsomely dressed in a red suit.

"Come, *habibi*," the man said, his voice now quiet and consoling. He led the child a few steps up the road in a move which seemed calculated to say that the two of them were in this together. Then suddenly Haroun turned back and shouted, "Come!", the word an order. "Come home *halla halla*, now now, or don't come ever. You hear me? Now or never."

She didn't come—Lulu, the second daughter of Abu Elias—and the man and the child walked on toward their house, a one-minute stroll across the road and down the hill.

Haroun and Lulu live on the top floor of a big cheap house, recently erected and still unfinished, on the site where his family has lived for generations. A part of the yellow stone wall of his father's house still stands a few meters from the bare concrete blocks of the newer wall. Each section of the house is lower than the other and has its own roof, so from our house it looks like broad steps going down the hill. Haroun's two brothers and their families live below Haroun and Lulu. And below his brothers lives his mother, Zahiya, alone, her husband dead all the ten years of the war. ("Luck to him," she says sometimes. "He didn't see all this shame.") A few steps down the hill from Zahiya's door is the little hut where her chickens roost and still farther down, where the ground levels off, the fields where she plants her vegetables and grazes her sheep.

In the afternoon the people of alien towns and forests across the canyon probably do not see our village as clearly as we see theirs. They have the light in their eyes. But the sun shines over our shoulders and pries into their streets, showing the buildings sharply drawn, the trees casting shadows, the rocks bulging. We cannot see the guns, but we know they are there. Toward evening when the towns are dabbed with blue and violet and shadows deepen in the forests, we can feel them there. But we have learned to forget things we know.

It was the best part of Sunday, the moment when the effortless slide toward evening begins to make me feel that it was a good day, that life is good. The man and the little boy strolled homeward; eavesdroppers on balconies, behind windows, turned back to their games, their conversations, and the bare-chested boy threw away the clean stick of his ice-cream bar and draped himself over one headlight of the postmaster's car.

I won the next round of Boggle, after he had beaten me three times in a row. When I read the word "injustice," Malcolm raised his eyebrows in surprise and said, "No, how can that be?" and then, "Well, there it is. Why didn't I see it?" Shaking up the letters for another try, he added, "That was easy for you. You see injustice everywhere you look."

"Me?"

"Sure. Emily, defender of the human race! Aren't you always on your soapbox? About how the innocent suffer?" He lifted the plastic lid from the box and turned over the timer.

I punched him in the shoulder to admit that I do often rage ineffectively, and, already scribbling on his paper, he said, "Look out. I'm getting ahead of you."

Again there was shouting down in the road, and we stood up. Haroun was back, his voice barking, and his pretty wife, Lulu, had come down to the street, fashionably dressed in a short white jacket with a lavender skirt that swished around her slender legs. She jerked open the door of Elias' dusty car, which leaned a little toward the bank of the hill.

"You are a fool," he said, shouting, though she was close enough to touch, "an ungrateful fool."

"You're right, you're absolutely right," she shouted back. "Only a fool would be married to a donkey."

"Meow," Malcolm said behind me, and I laughed before I noticed that it irritated me.

With a contemptuous flounce of her skirt, Lulu picked up the little boy and pushed him into the back seat of the car, where he became a red blob against the dark upholstery.

"If you go, you can't come back," Haroun said, as she slid across the front seat and under the wheel.

"Praise God! Praise God I can't come back to this hell."

"Where do you suppose she plans to go?" I asked Malcolm, meaning to forgive him for calling her a cat.

And he said, "She's not going anywhere."

Sure enough, before she could start the motor Haroun flung open the car door and snatched the child, while the bare-chested boy sitting on the postmaster's car watched, and the skinny lady who runs the village store came out to see what was going on. Down the hill, standing on the roof of her house, peering from under the shade of her hand, was Zahiya, as small and dry and shriveled as the okra she was spreading in the sun.

Just then Lulu leaped out of the car. Haroun stood the child on his feet, and he and Lulu began shouting, first by turns, then simultaneously, screaming into one another's faces and flailing their arms. Their voices grew louder, their words faster, the things they said unconnected and unintelligible.

I would like to say that I started to feel embarrassed at this point, embarrassed for my neighbors, making a spectacle of their anger, embarrassed for Zahiya who stood on the roof watching her son fight with his wife. But I was so curious that I only strained to catch the words they were saying. We were asking one another, "What did she say?" but neither of us knew.

And suddenly Haroun's hand, like a thing with a life of its own, struck her face, and her head jerked backward. My face stung; for no

reason it burned, and I put my hand on it. As Lulu turned away from
him, he struck her on the back. She picked up a rock, twice the size
of her fist, and held it beside her head and shrieked at him, "You are
a coward, a barbarian and a coward. You show your strength by
striking women and children. You are a beast, a filthy beast."

"Bravo," I thought. "Tell him. He can't knock you around like
that."

He was moving toward her, his hand raised, and she was backing
away, lifting the stone with difficulty, and I could see before she
threw it that she would miss him. He grabbed her by the shoulders
then and began shaking her, wobbling her head violently.

Other women came out of Abu Elias' house and began shouting
from the patio. The little boy was crying. From all directions people
were converging on the scene. Haroun released Lulu and started to
walk away, stomping in disgust. She screamed at him again, then
looked around, becoming aware of spectators. How could she face
them tomorrow, I thought, seeing her eyes dart from the people in
the street to the people on balconies. Doubling her fists and beating
the wind, she shrilled, "You shame me before the whole world," then
she lunged, pouncing on him, slapping and clawing.

A young woman among the spectators grabbed the crying child
and ran up the road with him, and two men moved in on the fight.
One took the husband by the arm and began steering him away,
speaking to him quietly. The other held Lulu's arms behind her.

"That's George," Malcolm said, peering over my shoulder.
"He's her cousin."

"He's good-looking. Why do I never see him around here?"

"He's a university student. I think he just comes from West
Beirut on the weekends."

At that moment Abu Elias came down the steep path from his
house, his khakis flapping around his spindly legs. He came hurriedly,
with purpose, though I did not yet see what that purpose was. He
said nothing. He ignored the sullen husband, being led away by a
neighbor. He walked like a man who owns the street, through the
crowd toward his daughter, who when she saw him coming kicked her

captor's shins in an effort to escape. George stepped aside, still holding one of her arms, just as Abu Elias slapped her.

I could see that suddenly the peacemaker's role became more complicated, for in the village doesn't a man have a right to beat his own daughter? But here and now? And as the young man tried both to restrain Haroun's wife and to protect her from her father, he also tried not to oppose Abu Elias directly, and the three of them began moving in circles, Abu Elias chasing Lulu, George trying to stay between them. In spite of him, Abu Elias was beating her wildly about the ears, the neck, the shoulders and occasionally on the seat of her pretty lavender skirt. At the same time she was screaming and trying to strike him back, a thing not permitted, and the young man took numerous blows, some from one direction, some from the other. They twirled farther and farther up the road, the dust from their feet making a little cloud around them, the whole village watching.

All at once she was on the ground. I wasn't sure how it happened. I blinked, and then she was lying in the dust on her back, her arms fallen crookedly around her head. She lay motionless, and the chattering and screaming stopped. In the hush I thought, "She is hurt. Oh no, she is really hurt! It is all silly, something we could have laughed about later, and now it is turning into a stupid disaster." I even said aloud, "She's hurt." And then I thought, without saying it, because the thought was so new and unfounded, that she was clever to end it this way. How could it end with her standing in the street in front of the whole village, having been beaten by both her husband and her father, having threatened to run away and failed, having made a fool of herself? The best thing was to get hurt, to faint, to pretend to faint if necessary. But she lay still a long time, and I said, "I think she's really hurt," and Malcolm moved to another window so he could see better.

As for Abu Elias, he turned and stalked back up the path toward his house, with the air of a man who had done his duty. I wouldn't have minded seeing somebody beat on him for a while.

George stood over Lulu, leaning to look down at her. His mother arrived and squatted to touch Lulu's face gently. Another of

Abu Elias' daughters, the plump older one, who had been watching from the patio, came down the path quickly, her rump bouncing a little, and ran toward the woman on the ground. Without hesitation she grabbed her sister by the arm and jerked her into a sitting position. Lulu flopped up like a rag doll, her head hanging forward, and then sagged into the dust again. The skinny, snaggle-toothed woman who runs the little store joined the sister, and they seized Lulu under the armpits and tried yanking her to her feet. Her legs were flimsy like strings, and she slithered from their grasp to lie in a heap. After that the sister sat on her heels holding Lulu's wrist and moaning, and Um Elias, their mother, came down the path carrying a glass of clear liquid with a spoon in it.

Malcolm said, "Wait until she starts yelling."

Just then she did, at two children who were trying to follow her. They stopped. "Go back into the house," she said. They did not go back, but neither did they follow her. They stood rigid on the path staring, sorrow and fright and curiosity in their faces.

Um Elias waddled up the street carrying the glass, looking at nobody, her dress like a sack around her ample body, her sandals slapping the ground. But before she reached her daughter, lying in the street in her Sunday dress, George suddenly scooped Lulu out of the dust, turned his back on all of us and disappeared around the curve, with her feet and her head dangling on either side of him. His mother followed them up the hill.

The men on balconies sat down. The skinny lady went back to her store. Zahiya turned and leaned over her okra, as the bare-chested boy slid off the postmaster's car and drifted down the road. Lulu's mother was still standing, undecided, in the middle of the road when there was a boom in the distance, around a curve, over a hill, and then a thud we could almost feel, and the deep, ugly rattle of a gun. Malcolm reached for the radio.

Fifteen kilometers away in a suburb of the capital, soldiers of the national army were trying to quell a street fight. The disorder started, some people said, over a silly thing. Muslims were tacking up pictures of their leader in a Christian neighborhood. Others said there was an attempted coup d'état. Either way, somebody fired machine guns and rocket-propelled grenades at the soldiers. The army, consequently, invaded the whole area in personnel carriers and went from house to house finding illegal arms and ammunition. In an adjacent part of the city hundreds of armed men appeared in the streets wearing hoods over their faces. An antigovernment militia group in the mountains began firing artillery in support of chaos. Shells fell on most of their enemies and some of their friends, as well as among the pretty pines on the lower edge of our village. Within two hours the noise of battle covered the earth.

George and his mother, Lulu, Haroun and their little boy, Abu and Um Elias and their daughters, all ran together to the shelter. "I guess they had to choose," Malcolm said, "between being mad and being safe." (Old Zahiya never goes to shelters, the first reason being that she cannot breathe in a closed room, and the second being expressed as a shrug and a prayerful turning-up of her hands. "We are under the will of God.") Malcolm and I made our bed on the floor in the inner room of our sturdy rock house. We lay close together, listening and sharing in whispers little bits of interpretation of the battle. "That's going out." "That's a mortar."

I said, "Why do you suppose they fight so much?"

Sleepily, he said, "You know as much as I know," and then I realized that I hadn't said I was thinking of Haroun and Lulu. He went to sleep in spite of the gunfire, and I thought all alone that words like they had shouted would kill me, the same as bullets.

The night was long and grim, the morning bitter. At dawn bright flames were eating black holes out of the forest. Around us on the mountains shells popped out of metal tubes, and the sound was like a great fist punching holes in the sky. The ground did not cease to shake all morning. Newscasters read the names of the dead and wounded. The president of the country said that the leaders of this foolish rebellion were not brave enough to come to the palace and talk about what they wanted. Politicians shouted into microphones, "They show their strength by attacking our homes. They are barbarians. They are beasts."

In the dead lull of Monday afternoon Zahiya trudged up the hill to visit me. She came with the dust of the fields on her skirt, walking on the backs of her shoes. Her hand was hard and strong, her face ancient. She asked about my health again and again, while sitting on my couch drinking tea, smelling faintly of animals and wood fires and wild herbs. She asked about my children, wished God to keep them for me, wished them to come home safely. Her mouth puckered around her gums.

She said, "Were you here yesterday? Did you see that *mushkale* in the street?"

A *mushkale* is a problem, but the distaste in her voice made it a shameful mess.

From the chair at the end of the coffee table, I passed her a plate of cookies and said, "Yes, I saw it." Then I added quickly, "It was a bad day for Lebanon. Everyone was fighting."

Actually I was thinking that events in the village, in Zahiya's family to be exact, made the rest seem unsurprising, but I failed to say it, and anyway, she didn't come to talk about civil war.

She said, "Have you ever seen anything so disgraceful? Have you ever seen a wife beat her husband in the street?"

I thought of reminding her that the wife had been beaten first and last, but instead I just said, "No, I haven't, but what can we do? When our children are grown they live their own lives."

She said, "They have no sense, Haroun and this woman. They are crazy." She touched her head with her finger and repeated, "Crazy."

Surprised, at a loss, I looked into my teacup and said, "I hope they are finished with the *mushkale* and everything is O.K. now."

She pulled her skirt lower around her knotty legs and leaned on her knees. "What do I know?" she said. "I'm not speaking to them."

Because I was not ready for this remark, I experienced a vague unease, then an impulse to say something, a fear that saying it would be rude, and finally a queasy, sinking weakness that probably ought to be called cowardice. While I was trying to remember when I had felt like this before, she added, "Luck to his father. He didn't see this shame."

That night Malcolm, who has a clean conscience with all of its rewards, wanted to sit on the roof and watch red tracers arching across the canyon. Standing at the top of the stairs, his wet hair brushed back, wearing pajamas and slippers, he called me, the way he might call me to see a nice moon, but I was depressed and half-convinced that somewhere a bullet or a little piece of a shell was looking for me. I waited for him down in the inner room, sitting on the rug and leaning against the rock wall, thinking while I waited about the inevitability of this useless war. I, reputed to be a campaigner against injustice, was thinking how logical, how reasonable and fair are our predicaments. But I may have been unjust to us all.

Months later, telling war stories at home in America, I mixed up the details of that particular stage of the civil war. Malcolm stopped me, looked at me with concern and said, "No, Emily. It didn't start in the street in front of Abu Elias' house."

To excuse my confusion, and then to cover my sudden comprehension, I forced a smile and said, "All these battles start to run together in my head."

The Deserter

I have come to Dorfweil to be alone. I traveled all night on the deck
of a boat with four hundred refugees who stampeded aboard and
squabbled over the blankets. I caught a cold. On the plane I slept
while my ankle swelled grotesquely. I hobbled to a train, carrying my
suitcase. I found a bus. When I signed the hotel register, my hand
shook only a little. "Lebanon?" the man said, and I turned away from
the surprise and curiosity in his face, knowing suddenly that my hair
drooped into my collar and my skin was gray. At last I entered this
strange room with the relief one feels on reaching home and locking
the door after being followed through the streets. It's true I checked
the corners and the closets, but after that I sat down in a stiff orange
chair, propped my foot on the coffee table and folded the quiet
around me like a comforter.

My room is clean and light. It opens onto a balcony with red
geraniums in the flower boxes and beyond, on the opposite hillside,
the picture-perfect village of Dorfweil. A hundred tall German
houses are clustered around a church, a church with slate-gray steeple
and towering windows. Below the church there is a garden where the
flowers form bright rectangles of color. Everything is tidy in
Dorfweil. Nothing seems to move.

It often seemed to be the clutter that was driving me crazy—a
new surprise every hour, squawking radios, broken concrete, tangled
wires, crying children, and the leaflets, arrogant orders on leaflets,
fluttering like snow through the air.

My retreat here is something like the German notion of going
away for a cure. At least that's what I like to think now that I am here,
that I have prescribed it for myself because I have been angry too

long, because I have lost so many connections between results and reasons, between words and meanings, because I have forgotten how to say the acceptable answers to questions.

I realize there is another way of looking at things. I have deserted. I have run away, when there is no escape for them, my pupils, my neighbors. It is a good sign, though, that I have come to a hotel. My impulse was to keep running, maybe to someplace where the roads peter out. I remembered a little cave in the hills of Virginia, and the thought was scary, because it was alluring.

Here in Dorfweil I go to the dining room three times a day. I share a table with an elderly woman who greets me enthusiastically in German. I speak to her in English, and it doesn't matter if the words come out wrong, as long as I nod and my tone is right. When she passes the bread a solicitous question rises with her voice and her eyelids, and the answer hums in my throat. There must be some primal language we all understand and will revert to when civilization is destroyed. All our towers broken down.

In front of my place is a little paper sign that says, "Frau Henry." At first I didn't realize that it meant me. Then I laughed and thought that maybe it is possible to be someone else, here in another country, to be Frau Henry, vacationing, laughing, and not a refugee, not an angry dropout or a casualty gone fuzzy in the head. I think about it over cold meat and fried potatoes.

Back in my room, I lock the door and drink the privacy, measuring joyfully the gray empty hours stretching in front of me. I deliberately do not remember anything, so I am always aware of the things I refuse to remember.

As the freighter pulled in the ropes and floated away from the dock, planes were roaring over us, low, and dropping their bombs on the city. We were sliding away from the noise and the smoke, when one of the planes, imperious like a bee, peeled out of line and circled us. The mob on the deck began to groan and push, to run toward the rails and dive under chairs. A young woman, dressed in mourning, stood rigid and screamed, and another woman seized her and screamed back. I was not afraid of the planes, because one can't be afraid of everything at once, and I felt something about to break inside my head. I covered my ears with my hands to contain the explosion.

Afraid again of the pulse pounding in my head, I pull the covers over my face and plead silently, Help me! Help me not to hate the pilots, their favorite sons who fly the F-16s. My stomach begins to burn.

I am delivered by sleep. When it grows cold in my cave I wake, and it is raining in Dorfweil. The tall German houses stand patient in the rain. Trying not to, I turn and look at the corner behind me. It is empty, the carpet meeting the white wall, neatly, cleanly. My ankle aches. I think that it feels good to be injured, visibly, to hurt in a spot that one can touch. I can see that the wounded have their consciences saved, even though I would be embarrassed to tell that I sprained my ankle running to see a fallen plane. And there was nothing left to see anyway. I am glad for an excuse not to hike, glad for the rain, glad not to meet anybody on the paths.

I did meet a girl in the hall, a girl with an awkward misshapen body. She spoke to me brightly, something slippery and full of "s" sounds. I shrugged and told her that I don't speak German. She asked me a question I didn't understand, and I replied that I am American.

"American?" she said. She had long, stringy hair, sallow skin and a large flat forehead. She followed me, plucking at my sleeve.

"I am Sharly," I thought she said.

"I am Flo," I told her and escaped into the elevator.

He was a terrorist, the media said, "hired by the enemy to create confusion," but that was all assumption, and there are many enemies. He was walking up the street, hurrying, carrying this package extended in front of him awkwardly, trying to run. A man said to him, "What is that?" The boy turned away quickly, into the entrance of a building, and the explosion brought down the ceiling of the vestibule and destroyed the door of the elevator.

That night we saw his head on television, a battered head, torn raggedly from its shoulders. The police wanted to know "Whose head is this?" His mother recognized him immediately, I heard. And me. I knew him. For four days she kept fainting again if they let her wake up. All these weeks I've been explaining to myself how it wasn't my fault.

Another time a bomb fell near a little church, mangling a lot of people in the street and shattering all the windows for a city block. Afterwards when the members went to sweep the glass out of their church, they found a man's head in the corner and little bits of flesh clinging to the walls.

Maybe I was overly impressed because it was new to me—this tendency of human heads to become dislocated. I started expecting to find them, like golf balls in the grass, or dusty shoes in the back of a closet. Since then I've noticed, too, that sometimes when someone speaks to me the words make an empty, distant sound or the answer dissolves into a white silence in my skull.

Other times I speak but the words come out wrong; I reach for something simple like "important," and it comes out "impertinent" or "impetuous." Sometimes I see all three words in my head and can't decide which one I mean.

Everything I know is hopelessly jumbled. There was an invasion after somebody was shot far away in another country. The connection between us and the one who pulled the trigger is hard to find, but there is that other connection, which maybe needed to be proven to someone, that if killing starts it might not stop. The killing came up the coast, roaring like a tornado. Pickers under the cherry trees heard it too late; school buses were overtaken on the road. But somewhere in this story people were fleeing north ahead of the reasons. I mean long before that diplomat fell wounded and couldn't die in Europe, I saw women and children knocking down the door of an old building on Makhoul St. They were wearing winter coats. All the scenes are vivid in my mind, but cut up and in the wrong sequence.

For years no government would talk to the refugees, because they were terrorists. Or maybe I got that backwards. Roadblocks are among the things that confuse me. Ramzi was kidnapped at a roadblock, strategically placed to prevent kidnapping. Roadblocks are a custom. Once half the population killed the other half with roadblocks. Starvation is still possible in the mountains. We remember. Every murder is revenge, all the way back to the Egyptian Moses killed in the desert. The invasion was a traditional way of preventing the future from being like the past. Traditions are... immovable, because we never forget anything, or maybe because we never remember anything right. I don't know. The air raids were all alike every day, the same smoke in the same places, the same scenes reappearing in the nonsensical movie.

Maybe I will get myself organized again here in this room.

In my craving for simplicity, I brought with me here only the barest necessities of survival. I have my Bible, an empty pad and a pen. Maybe some of these are superfluous.

I sit here with the closed book on my lap and think about what is inside and what I should read. Something irrelevant preferably, something with both feet in some other century. Wisdom from outside the situation is what I need. Not the Psalms, I think, because I don't feel like singing, and no bloody stories. Not the sharp, unflinching words of Jesus, either. I guess I am not ready for Jesus.

I open to the book of Proverbs and begin with an unreasoned confidence that if I read long enough the facts will start to fall into place again, and I will stop seeing heads in the corners. In spite of this clear-cut purpose, my reading follows a zigzag pattern. I start in the middle of the book, irrepressibly. Or do I mean irresponsibly?

"Like a gold ring in a swine's snout is a beautiful woman without discretion." It is surprising how some of these proverbs fall like little balloons full of ice water. I flip the pages. I read, "A fool takes no pleasure in understanding but only in expressing his opinion," because these words are already underlined in my book of wisdom-from-outside-the-situation. Solomon was very witty, but his wit has barbs that catch in the conscience. I admit that I am extremely opinionated and that I have often talked too much, but now, I promise, my tongue has turned to stone.

My eyes wander sideways and exactly across the page I see, "He who justifies the wicked and he who condemns the righteous are both alike an abomination to the Lord." This saying is not very witty. I feel anxious and accused. The clock says twelve-thirty, and I am not hungry. I am thinking that maybe I have loved too much the homeless wicked whose heads are blown off. My stomach hurts. I put my sore foot into my shoe, cautiously. I start walking. I am thinking, How terrible to be an abomination! Deliver me from condemning the righteous who have countries and parliaments and fleets of F-16s. I hobble down the stairs, feeling that I have eaten a harsh purgative. My brains whirl around in my head. I must approach this matter more systematically. I must begin again and read from the beginning.

In the dining-room there is one crowd and two ladies. The two ladies sit apart from the crowd and smile and gesture and pass dishes to one another, reaching the length of the table for six. They turn German and English into tonal languages and then back away into the quiet, private activity of chewing and clinking silver against china. Across the room the crowd babbles in an unknown tongue, and the noise of so many forks and spoons striking plates makes it seem that they are eating very rapidly. Together this chatter and this clinking have the happy sound of irrelevant rain falling on the just and the unjust.

I feel a thawing inside. When I get to my room, I will write about that, about the musical rhythms of a peaceful life, the view from my window, the beauty of solitude. I will find some soothing proverbs about brothers dwelling in peace together, and the words in my head will get attached to the right meanings again.

A woman rises and carries her plate to the serving table. She walks in a tilted stagger because of a twisted foot; the plate tips dangerously on a half-withered arm. On her face is an expression of pure delight. I am embarrassed without knowing why. Nevertheless I watch her stumble determinedly all the way back to her place. Across from her a boy who might be ten or twelve sits with his blond head hanging to one side. The woman beside him puts food into his mouth. His face is fair and handsome and blank. At the next table a man stands up to take off his jacket. He is chubby around the middle and has a paper napkin tucked into his belt, hanging in front of his lap. His face is lopsided and placid, his hair shorter than a marine's, and his vacant eyes bulge.

I forget to eat. I forget that it is rude to stare. A girl in a wheelchair leans slowly backward, her right arm dangling. I am alarmed that she will break her back or topple the chair. Nobody else pays any attention and suddenly she rights herself. I look away when she begins to lean again. A child who is pure idiot runs around the table on his toes, laughing. Now and then someone grabs him and hugs him.

If I were a complete stranger to Germany... In the *Bahnhof*, I remember, tickets were bought from a machine. Train information was posted, so the lady at the tourist information desk would not discuss it. I asked a uniformed man, "Do you speak English?" He said, "No" quickly and turned away. The crowd rushed by. I felt that the vast vaulted roof held indifferently the sound of marching boots... but in Dorfweil I could think the Germans are a warm and tender and boisterous, feeble-minded race.

The lady at my table, Frau Schulman, notices my scrutiny of the crowd. Knowing that I can't understand, she tells me something anyway; she explains. I feel stupid because I cannot reply.

The idiot child comes to the serving table and stands rubbing his fingers around in the clean dishes. His face is so flat I can look straight into his nostrils. His skin is pale and flawless. He laughs, a laughter full of mirth. When he lifts his hands and tosses back his shiny white hair, he is unexplainably adorable. For a moment I covet him, my neighbor's child. I could steal him and take him to my room. Oh! There is Sharly waving at me from a far table. Unintentionally I lift my hand, and my moment of sociability bursts like a bubble, like a cold balloon full of proverbs.

I am thirsty. We are eating fish, and I have no water. I talk about this in slow, careful syllables with the pretty girl who is floating back and forth between the kitchen and the dining-room. She wears a full, buoyant skirt with a ruffle around the bottom. She has blue eyes and roses in her cheeks. She understands that I want water but she insists that there is none. I am choking, and she explains to me politely the system. At the beginning of the meal one has a chance to buy a drink. I was late, but she doesn't say it in words. I can look around the room and see that people who came in wheelchairs and braces were on time. They have bottles in front of their plates. Finally I smile and say it is O.K. When I cannot bear it anymore I take my apple wrapped in a napkin and leave the room, aware that I am limping. No one can look at me and know that I am not part of the retreat for the handicapped.

Between me and the door a child is talking insistently, looking up at me, his head wobbling. Maybe he thinks he knows me. His sounds are all vowels as though he has no palate or no tongue. He tries very hard. I wonder if he needs a drink of water. I feel suddenly close to him—this stubborn German child. He is a survivor, a drooling, awkward victor over Hitler! He reaches to touch me, and I draw back from his hand. He is harmless. How wonderful to be harmless! But I cannot let him touch me.

I reach my room exhausted, and Sharly has followed me. She stands at the door, one shoulder lower than the other, her hips thrust too far backward, beaming at me until I let her in. This will teach me not to speak to people in the hall, or wave back in the dining-room. I want to read; I want to write; I want to be alone; and she is there on my couch asking me questions in slippery, sliding German. I tell her, "I don't understand," and when she finally catches on she slaps her face and says, "*O mein Gott.*"

She knows a few phrases of English. "I am fine thank you, come on, stand up please, sit down please." We repeat them endlessly. I try, "Go to your room," but it's plain she doesn't know that one.

We play a game of "What's This in English? What's This in Deutsch?" using the bed, the pen, the shoes. A light goes on in her face. She picks up my carelessly discarded shoes, squatting, with her back stiff, and places them evenly under a shelf. She takes my hand and leads me to the bathroom where we continue our game. The sink, the mirror, the hairbrush, the soap. We repeat all of these words after one another hesitantly, and I notice that neither of us is brilliant. We come back to the couch to sit down, and she is holding my hand. She has a distinctive bitter odor.

By acting out my words I communicate to her that I must read, that I must write, that I will see her downstairs in the room where we eat. She leaves saying, "Bye" after me and smiling uncertainly.

How jealously and selfishly I love this room, and the silence, and the words of the Bible and the blank pad of paper. And I read this afternoon from the ancient book something contrary to my idea. I read that wisdom is easy to find, that it cries aloud in the streets, that it raises its voice from the tops of walls and speaks at the gates of cities. I find this indeli... no, incredible and opposite to human experience. But I tell myself that I am not learning anything if I agree with everything I read. I think about the noisy streets, of music sensuous and discordant, the din of car horns clashing at an intersection, the sudden obscenity of gunfire, the call to prayer—a cry, on schedule, amplified, the rhythmic clacking of the corn vendor's spoons. And wisdom, where?

She is knocking at the door, Sharly. I ignore her and she goes away. She comes again and knocks harder. She tries the door handle. She knows I am in here, and I refuse to go to the door. I keep reading. I read and hear the words in my head above her knocking. I am a liar. Worst of all, I am lying to a child, a fourteen-year-old who is stuck at seven. I want to write but there is nothing to say. The foolish impulses I felt in the dining-room are dead.

All afternoon she comes back again and again, though I refrain even from running water or flushing the toilet. I walk barefoot on the carpet.

At six o'clock I can stand it no longer. When I open the door her face and voice are bright as ever. She chatters excitedly. I stand in the door and show her my watch. I point to the numbers and speak slowly. In half an hour I will come down to the dining room. I know she understands, because suddenly she weeps. And as suddenly I hate myself. Now I hate even myself and from hate and pity have taken her in my arms, the stiff brace around her body, her bitter odor.

At dinner a sense of shame clings to me. The feeling is a close acquaintance. Sharly's table is in the middle of the room. Mine is in the corner. Tonight she sits with her back to me.

Abdu always sat on the back row in eleventh-grade English. I had thirty-four eager and rowdy students. When I entered the room each day they jumped to their feet and shouted together, "Welcome, teacher!" And I had Abdu. He sat with his eyes lowered and thought about something else. If I spoke to him directly he answered in Arabic, which was against the rules in English class. The only piece of writing he responded to was an essay on Gandhi. He laughed. I became angry, because his laughter proved influential, and if the lesson plan ever got off the track in that class, I was in trouble.

Once he started talking I couldn't shut him up. He was speaking Arabic. His eyes were full of contempt. "You can't make Gandhi an example, not here, not for us. He was a citizen of a country. He was fighting arrogance and prejudice but not an air force. And he had time for demonstrations."

A chorus of agreement rang out, in Arabic. I made one last effort to be cool. I said, "Abdu, would you like to say that again in English?"

And he said in very plain English, "I'd like to say that again with a bomb. I'd like to put a bomb under this two-faced, preachy school."

The activity in the dining-room this evening is a distant hum to me. I'm afraid I'm ignoring Frau Schulman who always tries hard to make me a part of things.

I didn't think Abdu was serious, but it was as easy to buy a stick of dynamite as it was to buy an aspirin. I reported his threat to the principal, who expelled him. Long after I wasn't angry anymore I remembered the bitter expression on his face when he was emptying his locker, and my first faint flicker of remorse. There seemed to be still a trace of that rage, its blackness, its finality, on his dead face, on his bloody head in the middle of my television screen.

I guess he realized he had bungled the thing, whatever he meant to do, and tried to save the people in the street. One thing Abdu was right about. He didn't have time for demonstrations. A month later the whole community he lived in was rubble, and I was already ashamed to be a part of the world. It got even dirtier after that.

While I am eating my dessert Sharly comes and stands beside me. I say, "How are you, Sharly?"

She says, "I'm fine thank you."

I say, "Sit down, please," and she sits down. We smile at each other.

In the evening she brings a variety of people to my room. Gustave is tall and red-faced and has tiny eyes, far away behind his glasses. She commands him to "Sit down," "Stand up," "Go downstairs and bring Krompah," and he obeys, though he looks surprised and hurt.

It is Didma whose fair head hangs always to the side. When I say his name his whole handsome face smiles slowly, beautifully, and he begins to talk to me in elongated, innocent words which no one can repeat or explain.

Gertrude is there but giggles at her own private secrets and covers her eyes and puts her thumb in her mouth. It occurs to me that I am a little like her, and then I wonder why I thought such a ridiculous thing.

When Krompah comes he wears an expression of smug satisfaction on his thin face, perhaps because he has been called to our party. He has a baby hand attached at his left elbow and on the right a short arm with three fingers, a ring on the middle one. He is poised and smiling and talkative. Three times he shows me the ring and tells me that he has a girl in Cologne.

I seem to be learning German.

The others don't say "Sharly," I discover. They know her as Sylvia. I finally comprehend the explanation. (How patient they are in communicating with me!) Only at school is she called Sharly. Immediately I imagine a classroom full of children who are discussing an American movie about a half-wit called "Charlie."

Sylvia (isn't this more respectful?) tells the others that I read and write. Apparently she makes it sound like an occupation. Gustave and Krompah open my Bible and lean their heads over it. They gaze long at one page and speak with awe in their voices, because it is English.

There was a boy in one of my classes, so beautiful, so smart. At sixteen he meant to be a priest; at twenty he was a murderer many times over and more startled than I. He came to see me once after his militia group had been on an orgy of revenge. He looked very old.

"Remember?" he said. "I used to read my Bible every day." I didn't know what to say to someone in so much trouble. Now I hear myself thinking, May God forgive those who are past praying for themselves.

The children go to their evening songs, and I read the Proverbs again. I reread what I read in the afternoon, and it is all different this time, and all too late. The massacre is over. We have already eaten the bread of wickedness and drunk the wine of violence, and as the wise man said, "This way is a deep darkness."

Today their leaders are keeping the children busy. I am safe, but the pleasure is tainted by the feeling that I am hiding. I have done a lot of hiding. Often I lay awake listening to the whine and thunder of incoming death. Everything would be dark except for the fires, and I would lie there imagining that the shells were whistling in curving and zigzagging lines, hunting for the people all hiding in the dark.

Downstairs the stranded, I mean the retarded children are singing again. The tune is dimly familiar and disruptive. The words are German gibberish, but suddenly I recognize, "She'll be coming around the mountain when she comes." I think that she will, of course. Again. Whoever she is.

Sometime in the vulnerable days of my childhood we were singing in a cold schoolroom. Our teacher, in the middle of that song, glanced toward the window, a wistful absence showing on her face. She had red hair that lay in waves around her head, and the gentlest eyes. It hurt, knowing that she wished she were somewhere else. I sang as loud as I could, trying to make her see me.

The children are singing in German the repetitive words of that silly, eternal song, and I think how life keeps curving like a mountain road, so that we get glimpses of where we've been, to be awed or sickened by where we are, and how history... I imagine that history keeps folding and folding around itself.

When I think it is time for their meeting to end, I flee. I take a walk, limping a bit, across a little bridge to the village. Dorfweil is a real place after all. A muscular woman, stomping in wooden clogs, is dragging a boy up the steps of a house on the seat of his leather shorts. The pharmacy smells like cough syrup and soap. (I pretend to be looking for an English newspaper, but I am relieved when there is none.) The flower garden below the church turns out to be a cemetery, each rectangle of bright colors a grave. I walk and read the tombstones. Good, reputable citizens here, of course, buried in their hometown, honored with monuments.

There were pictures in the papers after the massacre. The dead were sprawled in the alleys, some still in postures of running. They were thrown into trenches and covered hastily. Like the rotting produce of the gas chambers.

I walk between the regiments of flowers and struggle through a dialogue with Abdu about how we all got where we are and what to do. We agree that nothing goes backward around the mountain. We argue some. I ask, without discovering his answer: have you heard wisdom calling in the streets? Does it shout sometimes, over the barricades, from the top of a wall? Out of the rubble?

It is Sunday morning and I go to the common room of my own will to sing the *Guten Morgen* song with the young people. There is a little boy who sticks out his tongue at everybody, and Gertrude has stopped one ear with an arm and the other with a finger. She clearly doesn't like the world.

Sylvia is thrilled that I have come and in her happiness runs to this person and that, chattering. And I decide that because I have made her happy I can slip away and be alone with the old, wise words and my demons. I can feel something working out now, if only I could think and put it all together.

Sitting at my narrow desk, I become so hopeful that I begin moving my pen in small circles just above the paper. Perhaps if I start writing words, any words, they will fall into a pattern, define the sickness that drove me here or tell me a way out.

It is Sylvia at the door, and I go back meekly for the "singing," because there will be Sunday worship and it is not appropriate to stay in my room alone, and because the noon meal will be the end of the retreat for the handicapped. After that I can write.

The chairs are arranged in a double circle around the big room. We are on the front row, and Sylvia never lets go of my hand. Probably she doesn't trust me anymore. She has wrung from me a promise to write to her and has written her address, barely legible, on a small pad in my room. (When she realized I would write in English, she slapped her face and said, "*O mein Gott!*") My address she carries, along with some coins, in a tiny purse hung from her neck. Every few minutes she checks to make sure it is still there. She takes it out and unfolds it and each time we go over the words and numbers together. It will be worn out long before she ever uses it.

Krompah is on the other side of me. He has twice shown me his ring and told me that he has a girl in Cologne. Now he says, "Oh, here comes the cross." I understand because just at this moment a man steps through the door carrying two gnarled branches tied together to make a cross. He makes it stand up by lashing it to the leg of a table at the front of the room. It is a crooked, knobby, prickly-looking cross.

"*Vundervah!*" Krompah says.

A procession of children marches in carrying their artwork— bright crayon sunrises, a papier-mâché elephant, a rabbit made of cotton balls. The little boy who puts out his tongue has covered his paper with a chaos of colors. A tall teenager has drawn skillfully a whole mural of wild animals. His giraffe has remarkable dignity.

They lay their work on the table like an offering, and now they bring many candles and light them and Krompah says again, "*Vundervah!*"

Across the circle from us Didma's mother takes a tissue from her purse. Her son's blond head is hanging, his face angelic; again and again she wipes her eyes.

Once when the country had fallen apart and so many people had died, I went to a concert, where the choir sang, "Thank you, thank you, thank you," and the audience cried, all of us, as though we had been waiting months for the chance.

A group of people stands up to read the Bible, one by one, and an extra boy joins them and reads what he wants to read at the end, so when there is applause it seems to be all for him, and he is proud and happy.

I have no idea what the priest is saying. He is walking up and down with his hands behind him, wearing khaki pants and a cowl which looks just like a brown pullover with a hood. Sylvia is holding my hand, and now and then Krompah nods, his thin mouth pursed in his characteristic expression of happy satisfaction. All around the room the retarded and twisted children are still and listening. My eyes travel from one face to another around the circle and suddenly, for a moment, I see myself. I am a misfit, ignorant, in need, and these children have taken me in.

At lunch, Sylvia leaves her place and comes to stand beside me. I say, "How are you, Sylvia?" and she answers, "I'm fine thank you." I say, "Sit down, please," and she says, "No." I look up at her, and she says in German, "You will write to me?" I say, "Yes," but avert my eyes when I see in her face the world's insatiable need to be loved.

She leaves the dining-room, and though I feel her waiting for me, I stay until Frau Schulman has finished her ice cream. Then I find her a few feet from the door, with a pale and frightened face. She throws herself at me, and even after everything I am surprised and bewildered by all those tears.

It's very quiet now in Dorfweil, the way I wanted it to be. Sylvia has gone back to school where she is the only one who doesn't know why she is called "Sharly." Even Frau Schulman left this morning. My ankle has shrunk to its normal size. I have started to feel a little guilty about lying down in safety, alone, a little ashamed to sit here feeding on ancient wisdom, with my feet on a stool.

I have read the Proverbs through. They are good news and bad news from a far country, and as Solomon said about the words of the wise, it is pleasant to keep them within you. It is pleasant on the whole, with bitter moments.

My retreat will soon be over. I realized that this morning when I read, "Like a lame man's legs, which hang useless, is a proverb in the mouth of fools." I read it and at that moment saw Sylvia with her stiff back and her stringy hair, her childish hopes dissolving at my door. While I read proverbs.

I have, through all these days, clutched a pen in my hand and have written nothing. Except a note to Sylvia: "Dear Sylvia, I hope you didn't get too tired on your long bus ride. Today the sun is shining in Dorfweil. I miss you. I am going home tomorrow. I will write to you again from Beirut." She will find someone who reads English.

I have a few more hours. Surely in this time I can form one sentence that will rescue some coherent thought out of all the irrelevancies of this retreat. I am not very ambitious. One idea will do, just something I can say when the plane lands to explain to myself why I came back.

Along the streets of that dear, wicked city, the walls will be broken, the rubble heaped. Sandbags will be wet and bursting at the roadblocks. There will be gunfire sooner or later, and a new class waiting for me behind their desks. When I enter the room they will rise and their voices will ring out, "Welcome, teacher!"

Princess Hala

All my daddy ever wanted was a son. That's why he married my mother, as far as I know. That's why I, baby number six, was born. Because he hadn't got a boy yet. I used to think I hated him for this, but then he got what he wanted, and with it the biggest disaster in the country. Maybe he deserved that, but none of us have ever said so out loud. Finally he stopped talking about having a son. He almost stopped talking at all for a while.

Tomorrow, Daddy's getting rid of one of his daughters. Maya is getting married, and Daddy is so thrilled he's half-crazy. He's spending money he hasn't got, painting the house, repairing the curtain rods, sending all of us to get professionally set and combed and plucked and manicured, and, of course, saying silly things. For example: "If we do this show right, it should result in some more proposals." He gets naive ideas like that.

That's why I went to the *nataafeh* for the first time yesterday. All of us have to dress up and look well-groomed. I'm not in the wedding or anything, because Maya has enough sisters without me and doesn't need a fourteen-year-old bridesmaid. But I have to wear heels and stand up with the family for pictures, so she said, and even Daddy said I had to get the hair off my legs.

Ordinarily my sisters do this at home. They cook a pot of sugar 'til it's dark brown and sticky and rubbery. They keep it in the refrigerator, in a covered dish, and when they want it, they warm it up a little and pull it and stretch it and break off pieces to stick on their legs. Then they yank the stuff off and yelp and stick on some more and squeal. It's very funny, except when it's my legs.

I went to the *nataafeh*, but not with my sisters. They made an appointment for us all in the afternoon; so I slipped off and went alone in the morning. Afterwards I had some explaining to do, and I couldn't say the real reasons. At first I didn't even know myself. I thought it was because of Tony getting killed the day before. I felt like the world should stop, because of that, but everybody kept on buzzing around getting ready for the wedding. I needed to think and I needed to cry, but there is no place to do either, not in our house, maybe not in the world. But I probably would have run off like that anyway. It gets tiresome, see, being the youngest sister. When I'm with any member of my family, I get treated like a child, but when I do things on my own, it's different. Adults like me sometimes, when I can speak for myself.

What I do usually is I pretend. Like yesterday, especially yesterday on the way to the *nataafeh*. I pretended that I was from a really good family, with a successful father, and a smart brother. I made it up that my sister was having a big wedding, and since I am her only sister I would be marching in ahead of her, carrying a bouquet of flowers flown in from Holland. I didn't plan to actually say any of this, of course, because once at school I claimed not to have any brother at all, and I was caught lying. Somebody always knows, see.

There's this girl who goes to my school. She's sweet, and I like her, though she's a little odd and says really weird things sometimes. Like me, she didn't get an invitation to Ahlam's big party to welcome her American cousin who came for a visit. I said I hoped there was a battle so nobody could come. I said I hoped the electricity was off all day and the *kibbeh* spoiled and the ice cream melted, but this girl— Fadia is her name—sort of smiled and said, "It doesn't matter; I'm the king's daughter." I looked at her, thinking first, I didn't hear that right, and then, as usual, maybe she's a little crazy. But the bell rang just then, and we had to go to class.

Anyway, on the way to the *nataafeh* I imagined my daddy to be not exactly a king, but a really nice fellow who loves daughters. I built him up as more reasonable and modern than most men, so that it didn't matter to him in the beginning whether he had boys or girls.

He was educated, too, and he knew that you couldn't blame the sex of a child on her mother.

I even kept on pretending that Tony was my boyfriend and would be taking me out to dinner after the wedding. I didn't notice anything along the way, not smells or holes in the concrete or car horns or anything, though once I saw a funeral notice stuck to a store window, and I stopped suddenly, like I'd heard an explosion, and a woman in front of me on the sidewalk said, "What?" and I started walking again.

I said to myself that Daddy treats my mother like a queen, especially when she's pregnant. And once he started having daughters, he realized that it's a lucky house that's full of girls. And I added to the story, which I was making up in my head, that when finally he had a little boy, a handsome little boy, so smart and everything, we all felt he had been rewarded for his kindness and patience and were happy for him.

By the time I found the *nataafeh*'s salon, I was walking with my head up and feeling like a princess. Karimeh wasn't surprised to see me or anything, because most people just walk in without an appointment, and she didn't know I was part of the family group scheduled to come in the afternoon.

The general appearance of things was definitely a disappointment. I guess I thought her salon would be slick and light with lots of mirrors and pictures on the walls and special chairs, like the beautician's shop, and then it was nothing but the sitting-room of her apartment. Downstairs by the iron door there was a little sign, painted about a century ago. It was a bit crooked and had a couple of shrapnel holes in it, but when I saw it, the meaning of the word *nataafeh* hit me. Because on our street there's this hole-in-the-wall shop that sells live chickens. Their sign mentions that they have a *nataafeh*. In other words, they sell you a chicken, right, and then they kill it and pluck its feathers out for you. You can even kill your own chicken and bring it in to be plucked. So there I was with my self-esteem pumped up as high as the Risq Tower, and I was going to the *nataafeh* to be plucked.

Stuff like this is happening to me all the time lately.

Anyway, I go ahead and climb the stairs, and they're dark and not too clean. I don't mean they were trashy, but they just looked like they hadn't seen any water for a few years. Of course, you can't hold the individual tenants responsible for that; the whole world uses the stairs (and spits on them), but I was just observing that this was not one of those classy places where they pay a concierge to keep the stairs clean and the elevator running and stuff. I forgot to mention that there wasn't any elevator, anyway, so add that to the dark walls and the unmopped stairs, and I was glad to be going only one floor up. Of course, it was not much worse than what most of Beirut lives with, but I was still trying to concentrate on my privileged background.

At first I thought I was in the wrong place, after all, because a young man answered the door. He was wearing pajamas at nine-thirty in the morning and looked like he had only opened his eyes one minute before. He could have been good-looking, except that I don't like men who look lazy. Besides that, either his looks or the way he stared at me made me suddenly think about myself, my real self, a little-sister type in handed-down jeans, standing in the doorway with a pimple on her chin and a big math book at the end of her long arm. He shrugged, which I interpreted to mean that I didn't matter anyway, and gestured toward the salon and then shuffled his slippers into a little room off the hall. Through the half-open door, a mixture of damp, soapy smells escaped, and I glimpsed the edge of a washbasin.

Karimeh's salon, like I said, was just her sitting room. There were no mirrors and no pictures except one of a man with a long twirled mustache, wearing a tarboosh and looking grim. He must have been somebody's grandfather. By that time, of course, I was not expecting more, which was fortunate, because part of acting sophisticated, I've noticed, is never being surprised by anything.

There were several women there, but I knew which one was Karimeh, because she had to be the one sitting on the newspapers in the middle of the floor. A customer was perched on a straight chair with her skirt pulled up over her knees, and Karimeh was at her feet working with big, flexible hands. She looked up at me and said, "Welcome," and I just chose a chair and sat down, like I always go to a *nataafeh* and didn't need to ask questions or anything.

Near the back corner an old lady, all in black, was smoking the *argheel*, and the bubbles made soft noises, like music, coming up through the water. Between her and me in the row of straight chairs was another woman. I couldn't see anything but her shoes, since I didn't want to turn and look at her. Those shoes looked very tired.

The couch and upholstered chairs in the room had been re-covered and the covers didn't exactly fit, but everything was clean and neat. The plastic flowers on the table under the windows clashed with the design of the oilcloth cover, but I guess some people wouldn't notice things like that.

I remembered then what my mother said about Karimeh, that she is a good woman, trying to make a living for herself and her son, who is always supposedly looking for a job but never finds one. I don't know what happened to her husband. Lots of things happen to husbands.

Each customer pays only one dollar if she just has her legs done, and not many women bother anymore to go to the *nataafeh*. I mean there are razors now that don't cut your skin, or so they claim, and razors made especially for the heavy hair we admire so on men and totally hate on women, and there are electrical gadgets that pull the hair out by its roots. So the *nataafeh* has lots of competition, and if we always had electricity, probably her shop would disappear like tarbooshes and handlebar mustaches.

Karimeh sat with one leg tucked under her and the other stretched straight out on the floor. This visible leg was so white I couldn't believe it, and completely smooth and hairless. Logically this fits, since Karimeh is fair and has green eyes, and her face, too, is smooth—long, and calm-looking and perfectly smooth, though not young, but something about this leg struck me as abnormal. I kept looking at it while Karimeh slapped her sugar taffy against the calf of the customer and then tore it off. She worked silently, paying no attention to the little cries this woman made. One of the customer's legs was already finished. I could tell because it had red splotches on it, the way my sisters' legs always look when they are newly plucked.

I tried it once, though my mother warned me not to. She said, "Be a child as long as you can." I thought it wouldn't hurt so much, because I didn't have a lot of hair yet, but never mind hair, the stuff took my skin off. Everybody laughed at me. Yasmine, another one of my sisters, said, "Wait 'til the *nataafeh* gets hold of you." That's another reason I wanted to go by myself. When it hurt, I didn't want any of them to know.

The women were talking when I arrived about what happened the afternoon before, about two cars racing through the streets, screeching tires, blowing horns, stirring up dust, bumping over the corners of sidewalks. They claimed people were yelling and dragging kids out of the street, and finally the first car—these were expensive-looking cars, both of them—came to some obstacle in the street where one driver shot the other dead.

I already knew about it. The dead one was Tony. Handsome Tony, who used to stand in the doorway of his shop with his hands in his pockets and smile at me and say things, things I wouldn't dare tell my daddy.

His shop was the prettiest one in our neighborhood—a men's-clothing store. The clothes in the window were elegant, worn by mannequins that looked real. Maya's fiancé went inside once and was disappointed because of the high prices. He asked Tony right to his face why he didn't display any prices in the window. My mother says forget about stores that don't show their prices right away. But Tony was very clever. He said, "That isn't natural. I try to show you how you will look in these clothes. Would you walk down the street or stand around with your friends, wearing a price tag on your coat?" Selim thought that was ridiculous, but I thought it was a smart answer, something most people wouldn't think of.

I often imagine myself going out to dinner at Mounir's or maybe The Tivoli, sitting on the balcony looking down on the street, with Tony. Antoine I would call him, and in my imagination he wears a satin shirt and pleated trousers, like those in the window at Chez

Antoine, and makes witty, clever remarks. If I ever have a boyfriend, I want him to have pretty clothes and clean fingernails and to say something original when he talks.

Tony's store closed, just suddenly. People said he owed a lot of money, and the factories wouldn't supply any more clothes. But people can say whatever they want.

This woman, who was sitting in the customer's chair with one leg plucked and red, said she had seen the whole thing. I could tell she thought that made her important, though she tried to make it a complaint, raising her shrill voice and acting like she had been insulted.

"Just on the way home from the bakery," she said, "carrying bread for supper, one child with me, the other alone in the house, and these maniacs come tearing through the street in their big cars. I thought they were going to go down the hill by the stairs instead of on the road. I was jerking Fufu by his hand, looking for a hiding place. Finally, there was a truck unloading something, stopped in the middle of the street, so they were blocked, and then I saw that one of them had a gun."

The other women were sympathetic. The old one, who was still smoking and not looking too alert, stopped making the bubbling noise for a second and said, "Praise God for your safety."

And the one sort of beside me said, "See this life. If the bombs don't get us, the foolish *shabab* shoot us." The way she said this, all young men are foolish. I glanced her way and saw that she was clutching a sweater around her bony shoulders.

But the loudmouth wasn't through with her story. She said, "He fired several times fast, there was glass shattering, and I saw the man slump over the wheel of his car. The other one backed up to the corner, still holding the pistol out the window, and drove away." She gestured with her hands to describe this. Her face had just one expression, like she deserved to have a better day, and her voice had only one tone, shrill, but her hands kept moving and described, like a picture, the way the man drove with one hand and changed directions and sped away.

And the bitter one, the one who was cold though the day was hot, said, "He'll get away with it, you know. They get away with anything these days." From the corner of my eye I could see that she had a very narrow nose, with a little flat place along the bridge.

It was time for me to speak, to make an entrance into this woman-talk, so, remembering that I was somebody and attractive and intelligent, I said, "What a shame! Antoine was a very nice person and a smart businessman."

They all looked at me for the first time, except Karimeh, who just kept pulling taffy in her hands, smacking it onto the woman's leg and jerking it off again. The only thing she said the whole time was, "I'm almost through, Hannan."

So this Hannan woman said, "You know him?", emphasis on the you. I'm sitting right in front of her, and she sounds like she's talking to somebody in the next house.

"Of course," I told her, "he's the owner of Chez Antoine." I hoped to imply that the men in my family buy their clothes there.

The old lady was leaning back now, against the cushions. She said, "Yes, dear, it is a shame. He left a beautiful wife and two babies."

I was sorry she mentioned that, even though I knew it. The old lady, not looking at anybody, almost like she was talking to herself, went on about how they were innocent, which was true, of course. She said that like most wives, Antoine's wife knew little about how he brought home the money. Then she turned her old, cloudy-looking eyes toward the woman beside me and said, "You should know her, Maliky. She's from the Atweh family."

Maliky (Queen, what a name for a woman like that) adjusted her sweater over her flat chest. While she thought how to answer, she looked down toward that flat place on her nose. Her eyes were little and sneaky like a mouse's eyes. Finally she said, "I do, of course, but not well. We don't speak to that branch of the family, if we can avoid it."

Karimeh said, "Finished, Hannan. You can wash in the bathroom." This was good news, that we could wash the sticky stuff off in the bathroom, and I knew where the bathroom was.

Karimeh got up, and walked out, sort of clumsy, and I noticed her legs were heavy, along with being super white. She might have been slightly crippled, or maybe she was just stiff from sitting like that on the floor. She disappeared through the hallway, and the three of us sat for a moment, Maliky turning her head this way and that in jerks, avoiding other people's glances, the old woman sucking on the pipe again, and I folding my hands in my lap, on top of my math book, and wondering just how I had lost my way in that conversation.

Then the old one looked at me. She was round and soft and kind-looking, with her white hair like a bright cloud around her face. She said to me, "What is your name, pretty one?"

"Hala."

"And who is your father?" On purpose I had said only Hala. I did not want to say my father's name. Old people tend to know everyone. So I said only, "Brahim. We are from the Brahim family." There are lots of Brahims, some nice ones, I hoped.

"What does your father do?"

"He sells automobiles," I said, but I think I hesitated just a second before I said it. Really, he does sell cars, old cars which he salvages after wrecks and bombs, using pieces from one to fix another. I sat there thinking, God, if you're real, don't let them ask me what kind of cars or anything like that.

Just then Hannan came back, brushing drops of water off her black skirt. Everybody told her, *"Naeeman,"* because she was all smooth and nice now. I noticed then that she had a pretty complexion with glowing cheeks.

She said, "I heard the shooting was about a car."

Before anyone could answer, Karimeh limped in, carrying a tray of coffee cups and a little pot with a saucer over it. She dragged around some small tables, one for each of us, and while she was pouring the coffee this gorgeous woman, so sophisticated, arrived, all out of breath, and she saw the coffee and said, "My mother-in-law loves me."

I thought, Why do we claim that our mother-in-law loves us, if we arrive someplace just at the right time? We all say this thing, but no one ever told me why.

Karimeh called her "Renee." She said, "Renee, I thought you were coming tomorrow."

Renee had an explanation. She said, "Tomorrow is impossible. The dinner party is in the evening. I have three Sri Lankis coming to help me, and I can't trust them to do a thing without supervision."

So Karimeh said, "No problem, I have only Maliky and the girl ahead of you."

Renee acknowledged all of us and spoke to the old one, calling her Madame Zaitouny. Then she pleaded to all of us that she had to be done immediately, otherwise she would have to leave, because she must go to the florist and order flowers, so Karimeh asked our permission. Maliky said it was O.K. and I said, "With pleasure," and Karimeh sat down in the same position as before at the feet of Renee, whose legs looked great already. She was wearing a stylish pair of shoes with skinny heels and slender straps around the ankles. She opened her bag and put a cigarette between her bright-red lips, lighted it with a little silver lighter and leaned her head back as she blew smoke. The cigarette smelled pleasant, like a spice. My daddy's smell like burning garbage.

"What a nuisance," she said. "The pain we endure to be beautiful!" And she laughed. She looked stunning with her curved eyelashes and the soft green scarf at her throat and her smoking posture and her polished nails.

I wondered suddenly what it would be like to have a mother like that, so at ease, so (I think the word is chic). Because I look at my mother and I get scared. I love Mama. I want to fight my daddy when he speaks ugly words to her, but I think that if I stay around her too much I will be like her. I will be stooped and have a missing tooth and rough hands. I will be afraid to defend myself.

By that time I had forgotten to pretend that I was beautiful and clever. So I smiled at Renee and tried to recall the fantasy I built up just an hour before. I thought I should be talking more, but when I talked, people got curious about me and started asking questions. I didn't want that to happen, but watching Renee get her gorgeous legs plucked, I noticed again that wonderful smooth leg of Karimeh's, so

I became bold and asked her if she cleaned her own legs.

She smiled, and Madame Zaitouny laughed, and then Karimeh told me, "When I was a newborn infant my grandmother used an old secret that the village women knew. She put bat's blood on my legs, and on the legs of my sisters, too, when they were born, and none of us have ever had a hair on our legs."

Before I could understand this astonishing tale, Renee began to scream with laughter. "You are making this up, Karimeh. I can't believe it."

"No, believe me. They told me. My grandmother, my mother, my aunts. Apparently there was a time when a lot of people did this."

Renee's surprise agreed with mine and that gave me courage to say, "Then what happened? Why did our grandmothers not do that for us?" With a gesture I put Renee and me in the same boat. I could see us on the balcony at The Tivoli, her table near mine.

"Life changed. How would people in Ashrafiyeh get bat's blood? Besides that, would I tell?" Karimeh said. "If they knew how to prevent hair, I would be out of business."

Just when I realized we were having fun, Hannan spoke. I really wished she would leave, because of her shrill voice and her fake anger, but she had stayed to drink coffee, and she brought up again the shooting that she saw so she could tell Renee how she had been practically involved, having a curbside view.

Maliky said, "Does anyone know who did it?"

And it turned out that Renee, who was far away in her home on the mountain, knew more than Hannan. She said, "Oh yes, I don't want to mention his name, but the forces picked him up. They took him for his own protection, of course, because Tony and his wife together have a thousand relatives."

Gradually a big story came out. Maliky said that Tony always had money. "He had big cars, put his wife in a luxury apartment with Persian carpets everywhere, showed up in the best restaurants, frequented the casino." She said all of this sounding jealous and mad. Everyone knew, she added, that he opened a new business every few months and closed it shortly, and that probably meant that he took goods from the factory on consignment, sold what he could quickly and never paid.

"That's the rumor," I said.

Then I was disappointed, because the old lady said, "It seems to be true."

And Renee said, "It fits with what I know. He bought a car from the *shab* who killed him, a good boy from a very good family, and wrote a check for it. When the check bounced, the young man came back to him and asked for his money, like anybody would. Tony said, I don't have any. And the other fellow said, Then give me my car back, and Tony told him he didn't have the car; he had sold it to someone else. And the *shab* said, Then you must have the money, and Tony said, No, I already spent it."

"What a shame!" Madame Zaitouny said. "Now he's dead, and the other one is a murderer."

"Really, and he is a good *shab*. My son went to school with him. What could he do? He got robbed." There was a moment of silence and then she added, "He lost his head, of course, in total frustration, but he rid the community of a crook."

I could feel my face burning. I wished someone else and not Renee had said that.

Then Madame Zaitouny said, "Yes, Tony got what he deserved, I suppose." Her voice was soft and thoughtful, and she went on to express her opinion that people always pay in the end. I noticed that this was a contradiction of what Maliky said earlier, about everybody getting away with things, but really I was not thinking much. I could feel myself slipping into a very bad mood.

Hannan seemed satisfied at last. She told everyone to be careful, like she cared anyway, and then she left. That improved the atmosphere.

Renee rattled on about her dinner party. Some of the leaders of the forces would be there, a certain parliamentarian, her husband's business associates. She was doing all the food—salads and dips, *kibbeh*, a leg of lamb, a baked fish with walnut sauce, everything but the *osmaliya*, which would be delivered at serving time. There was nothing she dreaded like the crust starting to lose its crispness.

I kept picturing Tony, so tall and proper-looking in his powder-blue suit, like someone people could trust, and like I saw him once, in a white shirt with two rows of lace down the front, open a little low, exposing just a bit of black hair on his chest. Girls liked him, not just me, lots of girls, but I liked him more than anybody else did. I used to walk up and down the street just to get a glimpse of him.

I hate it when someone who is handsome turns out not to be nice. Mama told me more than once, "Don't make up your mind, even about a fig, from the way it looks outside." She always breaks open a fig before taking a bite, because sometimes there's a worm inside. That's scary. Once you see a little white worm in a fig, you lose your appetite for figs. I didn't want to think about worms or about Tony doing a dirty trick to that other *shab*, but most of all I didn't want to think about Tony slumped over his steering wheel with blood streaming out of his head.

My daddy says there is no such thing as justice. He says there's only luck, good or bad.

Renee left, and she was hardly at the bottom of the stairs when they started talking about her.

"She's filthy rich," Maliky said, "and I do mean filthy. Her husband made his money selling glass for two prices to all of us who got our windows broken by the shells. They support more than one militia group, you know. It's good business. The war stops, we don't need new windows so often."

"But that's how rich people get that way," Madame Zaitouny said. "They see opportunities."

"O.K., let them see opportunities, but they don't have to take advantage of the rest of us. And then brag about the parties they throw with our money."

And I said, "Probably, she doesn't even know how to make *osmaliya*."

Everybody looked at me.

I explained, "Mama says almost nobody knows how to make *osmaliya*. Everybody, including her, makes something they call *osmaliya*, but it's not the real thing." I just said this to show off, then I realized for the first time what it meant—that I've never actually eaten *osmaliya*.

For some reason I felt the need after that to say something good about Renee, so I said, "She's a beautiful woman."

Maliky snapped back, "Sure, and she agrees with you."

It seemed like a good time to be less conspicuous, so while Maliky got her legs plucked, I opened my math book. On Monday morning Mr Baz would give us a surprise quiz on percentages. I could feel it in my bones, like a disaster coming. I started flipping pages. The pages in that book always seem heavy, weighed down with all those math symbols. I found between them a little booklet that Fadia gave me. It turned out she meant something serious when she said she was the daughter of a king, so she gave me this to read, said it would explain, but I tucked it into my book and forgot about it. Not that I wasn't interested, but I forgot where I put it, and I don't look into my math book too often.

Maliky was talking about what bad luck she had had in her life. It was all because of the evil eye put on her by a certain woman. She had seen her do it. This witch who hated her had stood at the corner of the garden and stared at Maliky's mulberry tree, which always had big wonderful berries, up to then, luscious, sweet berries, almost solid along the limbs. She used to give them to all the neighbors and make juice which she served her guests. And from the day that woman stood and stared at her tree, it never bore fruit again. She had put a curse on Maliky and her family. It started with the mulberry tree and went on to other things.

If Maliky's story was true and if Madame Zaitouny knew what she was talking about, then that woman who put the curse would be punished. God would even things out. But if my daddy was right, then the world was just a mess and there was not much use trying. And, though I didn't want my daddy to be the winner, even in a backgammon game, I thought that his view of things had more facts behind it. Take my mama, for instance, she never got what she deserved. For all her love and her work and her patience, all she got was tired. After my brother was born she told her sister that she just wanted to walk out in the street and stand under the shells and die. She doesn't know I heard that.

The booklet I found inside my math book seemed to be religious. I saw the word God here and there. It looked boring. Then I noticed a heading over one of the pages. It said, "A Child of the King." I guessed this was the part I was supposed to read, so I started. It seemed more interesting than percentages, at least. The author was a woman, that was something, and she said that life became exciting and important after she discovered that God was her father and she was his daughter. I kept reading for a while, but I didn't understand how this works. I supposed it was like what happened when I was on the way to the *nataafeh*, when I imagined all these great things about my father and arrived feeling like a princess. That's what a daughter of a king is, a princess. I guess if your father is wise and powerful and rich, you won't mind much if people don't invite you to their parties. But in that case, how you feel about being slighted won't be too relevant, because you won't be. People will invite you to everything. Because of your father, even if they don't like you. I knew I was forgetting something—that God was the father in the book, but even with my love of pretending, I couldn't imagine having any strings on God. And even if I did I would still have this other father who hurts my feelings and embarrasses me, not to mention a freak for a brother, and a mother who wants to die. I wondered what Fadia would say to all that.

Suddenly Maliky was gone, and it was my turn to sit in the chair with Karimeh at my feet. The first time Karimeh ripped that goo off my leg, I started to wish I hadn't come, because it hurt like something crazy. All the time, I couldn't be quiet. I'm just a silly kid about pain. I'm silly in a lot of ways. I even loved a married man with kids, and he's dead now, anyway. But Karimeh and Madame Zaitouny started talking, and mostly I think they didn't notice that I was whining and sniveling and wiping tears with the back of my hand. What they were saying about Maliky was really shocking.

First Karimeh said, "She's had a hard life, poor thing."

And Madame Zaitouny said, "She brought it on herself."

"How's that?"

"Well, first she gossiped about everybody she knew. According to her, other people's daughters were loose and immoral. Other parents didn't maintain proper standards for their children. She said terrible things about the Khairallah girls because they sometimes went out with boys. She blackened their name in the whole town, saying they were not virgins. Then, wouldn't you know? Her son fell in love with the youngest Khairallah girl and wanted to marry her."

Karimeh drew in her breath. "What did she do then?"

"What could she do? She opposed him completely. He insisted, said he would never marry if he couldn't marry that girl. Maliky got sick and went to bed. The doctor said it was her heart, so finally the boy relented."

"*Haram*," Karimeh said. "Then what did he do?"

"He emigrated. To France, I think, and now she is bitter because he never comes home.

"And that's not all, her daughter left her husband and three children to run away with a hippie, at least I call him a hippie. He was a foreigner who came through here looking for drugs. They lived in a little room under the stairs of an apartment building for several years. He lay around numb, shooting stuff into his veins, and she scrubbed floors and had kids. I don't know where he is now. Some people say he left her, but I also heard that he got caught with no visa and was deported. Either way, she is still living there under the stairs, working as a maid to support her children."

"Poor Maliky. No wonder she always seems depressed."

Madame Zaitouny quoted a proverb then. She said, "You dig a hole for your brother, and you fall into it."

I paid my dollar, washed my skinned legs and my face, and left. Down in the street the traffic was snarled up like a knotted ball of string, so I walked between the beeping cars, angling across in the middle of the block or through intersections, wherever I wanted, looking at nobody. Everything was hot—the road, the cars. It felt like the whole sky was burning. I carried that math book, heavy as a tank of *butagas*. I smelled garbage, stepped over holes in the road and told myself the truth.

My father cursed on the day I was born. He cursed every time he was told he had a girl, but I know that when I was born that was the worst time, because I was number six. Maya remembers. She told me, but she didn't have to. I would know.

He has told us enough times how worthless girls are. "You support them, send them to school, and then they marry and belong to some other family. They are gold diggers. They are naggers. They never have everything they want, especially clothes. They are silly. They are always sick. They sit around the house, in the way, or else they disgrace a man by running around with boys. The neighbors gossip about what time they come home."

Examples to the contrary don't interest him.

The last time Mama was pregnant, Daddy paid a fortune-teller to read his coffee cup. She predicted he would have a son, and she was right. A few hours after he took Mama to the midwife, Daddy came home and started kicking doors and throwing things. We girls ran and hid and cried, while he nearly destroyed the house. We tried to understand. We asked him if the baby had been born. We asked him if Mama was O.K. He wouldn't talk. Finally, the house was quiet, and Maya sneaked out of the bedroom and found him gulping down a bottle of whiskey.

When Mama came home with the baby, we understood, even I, though I was only five. He looked like a monkey—from the first moment I saw him until now, when he is nine. You have to see to believe. Big mouth, with teeth jutting out. Two holes for a nose. Tiny eyes. They shine, but they're empty. Nobody home. Head sloping backward, small at the top. Hair all over. Flat like a monkey's fur. We would hide him from the neighbors, if we could. Long, long arms, with hands dangling near his knees. Hairy arms, hairy hands. He runs all the time—on his toes, in spurts. Did I say he's nine? Screams to get what he wants, though he did learn to talk a little when he was about seven.

That saintly-looking old lady with the halo of white hair

probably figured out exactly who I am. We must be famous for our jinxed father with his family of girls and his male monkey. While I was sitting there pretending to be privileged and wanted, she was working it out in her mind. By now she has told Karimeh everything, Now I realize why she was there, certainly not to get her legs plucked. The *nataafeh*'s salon is a place for women to talk, to gossip about everybody who isn't there.

That's what I was thinking on the way home.

The funeral notice was for Tony. I read it through. They must have carried him out of the church about the time I was crying at the *nataafeh*.

When I got home, the zit on my chin was bigger, and everybody was mad at me for running off without an explanation. I sat for a long time with my back in a corner and my math book propped on my knees, but I was reading that little pamphlet. All of it, from the beginning. I got a kind of a burning feeling in my chest when it described God. I came to the end and wanted more.

That was yesterday. In a few hours my sister Maya will be married, and she will not live with us ever again. Maya is very smart. She wanted to study computer science, but Daddy wouldn't let her go to college. Actually, he couldn't pay. Selim is an auto mechanic. All of us girls think he's cute. He has curly hair, a little long. He says funny things, too, and laughs a lot. I like him, except for the grease under his fingernails.

Daddy is satisfied. He knows it's not easy to marry off girls when there's a monster in the family. Today I had the crazy feeling that I wanted to hug him. I'm sorry that none of us could be what he wanted.

Mama has been slaving all week. Just because Selim's family will come to get the bride, she is washing windows and mending little tears in the bedspreads. She even made us clean out the closets. She runs from one job to the next, fidgets with her dress, telling us its tacky, and now and then suddenly sits down and cries. She once told Maya to run away and get married, so she wouldn't have to go to the wedding, but Maya wouldn't. Mama doesn't like weddings, not even strangers' weddings.

I think myself that it takes a lot of courage to get married. I told Mama this morning, while we were washing the glasses we borrowed to serve punch in, that I never would. I thought she would be happy, but instead she said I should put that out of my head and start looking for a nice boy. She said that whoever doesn't get a husband will get stuck taking care of our idiot brother when she is gone. The thought almost made me sick.

Life is very scary. Among all the wars we've got going on, there is the one between luck and justice, which I never really thought about until yesterday. Now I wonder if there is any reason why things happen the way they do. Does one thing create another? Does it matter if we're good or bad?

I've decided one thing, anyway. When the wedding is over I'm going to find out about this "daughter of the king" business. I mean, what if it's real? I'll chase Fadia and make her tell me. Maybe it's my chance to be glad without making it up.

Another thing; I've been thinking about bat's blood. There are still plenty of bats in this country, I guess. They live in caves in the mountains. Why couldn't somebody catch bats and bleed them? This idea is worth a fortune, and I gave it to Maya and Selim for a wedding present. It's our secret. They laughed at first, but I said, "That's how people get rich, you know. They see an opportunity and go for it."

Friends, Strangers, Brothers

Because Abdu lived by principle and refused to be stopped at the occupation army's checkpoint, Malcolm drove around the hill and down to the orchard alone, hauling the boxes they would need.

It was soon after dawn when they threw the wooden crates into the trunk and back seat of Malcolm's car, and Abdu set his clay water jug in the front seat and started walking down the slope. The morning was radiant, the sun spilling over the opposite mountain but not yet reaching the wadi, the forests still full of blue shadows. A flock of black goats clattered across the road, raised a cloud of dust, and started nibbling among the weeds and thorns. For a few moments Malcolm sat behind the wheel of his car, smelling the dust, the bitter weeds and occasional whiffs of manure, enjoying the expectation of simple work and the idea that he and Abdu could be a team, harvesting the plums. He watched his friend, tall and gaunt and deliberate, descending along a zigzag path, stepping carefully through a vegetable patch and skirting a vineyard before he dropped over the terrace wall and disappeared among the pine trees.

Malcolm spent most of his life behind a desk or a lectern, but he was drawn to men who tilled the ground and was secretly envious of those who worked in the sun and wore calluses on their hands. By the intelligence of such men, we all live, he thought, staring at the spot where Abdu had entered the woods, and behind the thought, a mere suggestion of fear slunk through his mind, the fear that economics professors did not contribute anything essential to the world.

There was nothing frightening or difficult about passing the roadblock as far as Malcolm could see. The soldier looked at him closely, then motioned him to proceed. Abdu's obstinacy seemed like useless pride, but because it was Abdu, Malcolm assumed he must have a good reason. For a year or more the farmer had not been to his own land by road, choosing instead to carry loads of fruit and vegetables up the mountainside on his shoulders.

The little road, which had been blacktopped years ago but was now full of chuckholes, wound through a snobar forest and down into the morning shadows of mountain bluffs, toward the little dirt trail that led to Abdu's plum trees. The pines, the fruit trees, everything looked small, because of the way the canyon walls hovered on both sides. Malcolm felt small.

By the time he reached the orchard, Abdu was there, walking around, inspecting his fruit, not looking small at all, but like a giant scarecrow with oversized hands, loose trousers, and a leather face slashed with crevices. Immediately the two men put the boxes on the ground under the first row of trees and began to reach into the branches to grasp the purple fruit and then to stoop and roll it off their fingers, gently, into the boxes.

They worked silently; none of their usual discussions of politics. If they were sitting at Malcolm's kitchen table or on Abdu's back patio, Malcolm would ask Abdu his opinion about the president's latest trip to neighboring capitals, even though Abdu's interpretations often seemed far-fetched to him. Actually, he didn't even like to talk politics, and he was aware that, just as Abdu's thoughts were illogical to him, his own were naive to Abdu. Yet they talked politics; it was a contagious compulsion, epidemic in Lebanon.

Right away the day grew hot. Bees and flies hummed, searching for broken fruit and oozing juice. Under the plum trees the air was still and heavy with odors—fruit, dust, vinegar, decay. Malcolm stood on a box more frequently than Abdu, because he was shorter. And Abdu, who never hurried and never wasted any effort, had filled his first box when Malcolm's was half-full.

"Slow down," the American said. "You're making me look lazy."

"Never mind, *Ustaz*. I'm used to this." Abdu always called him "professor," out of genuine respect for his education, but Malcolm could never find an adequate way to express his esteem for Abdu, a man his own age who always seemed both younger and older, more expert in the art of living.

They stopped for a drink from Abdu's jug, Malcolm already turning pink from the sun, and agreed that they were hot and there was a foulness in the air. For a while they went on working, but as the temperature rose, the impression of something rotten came on relentlessly, breath after breath, like a sinister shadow approaching through the trees.

"There is something dead here," Abdu decided, his nostrils quivering. And as he finished the branch he was stripping with his big hands, he began to glance over his shoulders and between the rows.

"Maybe a dog?" Malcolm said, and finally Abdu ambled, stooping under the limbs, to the end of the row. Malcolm saw him lean to peer at something on the ground, then motion for him to come.

As Malcolm approached, Abdu spoke softly, "It is not a dog. Come see."

Malcolm followed him to where the soldier lay among the clods and stones and summer weeds. His mouth was open, as if he had called for help or cried out in pain. Death had made the gesture gross by preserving it. A fly buzzed in and out of the blue cavity. Though his body was expressionless now, like a stone or a jar, a thing, an empty thing, he could not have been dead many hours. Youthfulness had not yet departed from his face. His uniform bore the insignia of the occupation army.

Abdu and Malcolm stood over the body and looked at one another. They began to speak in whispers, their voices smaller than the insects'.

"How did he get here?" Malcolm asked.

"I don't know."

"Who could have killed him?"

"They kill them," Abdu said. "The militias. Every night one or two."

"Was he shot?"

"I don't see the wound." He leaned, pinched the soldier's sleeve in his fingers and lifted the body until they saw black blood on the back of his shirt. "Here it is. Knifed in the back, but I think it happened somewhere else. There's not enough blood here."

"Look in his pockets. Does he have an I.D.?"

Abdu dropped the dead man's sleeve, and the body rolled back like a log. "We don't want to know who he is."

"Why? What must we do?"

"We have to hide him, get rid of him."

"But shouldn't we report it to someone?"

The sudden lifting of Abdu's eyebrows would have been answer enough, but he added, "My sons are in the militia, and this body is on my land."

"Waleed and Hanni would be...?" He wanted to say "implicated," but his Arabic failed him, so he said, "Would be in trouble?"

"Of course. Big trouble." He turned his back and with a gesture called Malcolm to follow him to the place where they had been working. He started picking plums again. "I have to think," he said, "but keep picking plums."

His long, leathery face was expressionless and calm, and Malcolm remembered the day when they were sitting on Abdu's patio, drinking mulberry juice, and heard a shell come whistling across the canyon in front of them and crash nearby. Malcolm had tensed to leap from his chair, but Abdu had not even blinked. He had pointed to a billow of dust on the far hill. "The gun is over there," he said. And jerking his thumb toward a burst of smoke on their left, "The shell hit there."

Abdu rolled a handful of plums into the dark heap in the box at his feet, stood up and said in a loud whisper, "Listen. These soldiers get ambushed at their posts. Sometimes they just disappear. I don't know who does it. I know, but not specifically who. You understand?"

"The militias are trying to drive them away, I know. But what are we going to do?"

"I'll go for kerosene. We'll burn it."

"But if you and Waleed or Hanni went to the army and reported the body, wouldn't that prove they were not guilty?"

"It would prove nothing," Abdu hissed. "They are guilty whether they did it or not."

"Wouldn't it be better just to bury him, then?"

"This ground is too hard and rocky. We couldn't put him deep enough. And we don't have that much time."

Malcolm knew finally that Abdu was afraid and became afraid himself. Soldiers were camped around the curve of the hill, a kilometer away, the same soldiers he had driven past two hours ago and must drive past again today. Even now they might be looking for this man.

"Stay," Abdu said. "Stay here, pick plums. No. Find sticks, dead branches, anything. Cover the body. Then pick plums. No one must know, *Ustaz*. No one."

Malcolm expected him to leave running, but he began to walk with his usual calm dignity, except he hesitated once, came back and hoisted a box of plums onto his shoulder.

Malcolm began darting this way and that, grabbing anything burnable in sight. Abdu was right; it was the only way. They owed nothing to the enemy, not even to such a young enemy. But he was already feeling dirty and deceitful, because of Emily. He could not tell her about this. She had reflex feelings about lost soldiers, understandably. She would get upset, and no matter how he explained it, he would go down another notch in her eyes.

This is how it happens, he thought, that honest people develop lists of things they can't talk about and start hiding things about themselves. As he thought this, he was searching for broken limbs and tearing at the brown thornbushes, trying to pull them up with his bare hands. There was so little brush, and before he had half covered the body, he heard voices and rushed back to the other end of the row and began picking plums again. Two men were coming, one of them calling Abdu.

"Welcome," he greeted them, trying to be casual and cheerful. "Abdu is not here; he went up to his house." His voice trembled. He was sure it would betray him. The smell was obvious now. Could one talk enough to keep people from noticing a smell?

One of the men was a local taxi driver, whom Malcolm recognized. He stood with his hands in his pockets, jingling his car keys. "My passenger needs to see Abdu."

The other was a short man, shorter even than Malcolm, who tilted his chin up and looked at the world through half-closed eyelids. This habit made him appear to be suspicious. The two men stood there, watching him pick plums, listening to him talking, too much and too fast, saying that they had just missed him, and he would probably be gone for quite a while, and Malcolm became self-conscious about his movements. He was not experienced in harvesting fruit; maybe this was evident to them. Then the short man with the suspicious eyes said, "Something smells bad here."

Malcolm thought, I knew it. A Lebanese will never miss a smell, especially if it's bad.

He said, "Yes, there is a dead dog."

Then the taxi driver took a couple of steps toward the inside of the orchard and said, "Or maybe..."

"Never mind. We found it. Abdu went to bring kerosene so we can burn it."

The driver turned around, took his hands out of his pockets and said to his client, "We'll catch him up the hill." It sounded like he was saying that they were obviously unwanted.

Malcolm could feel his heart pounding in his throat; he was not sure he had said the right thing. He kept picking plums, in case they should look back.

Once he had brought home a bone from the rubble of Tel azZatar, a thighbone. It was long after the battle there; sunshine streamed in through devastated walls, and silence filled the little tunnels where people had hidden during the siege. Emily had been horrified that he would handle it, would bring it into their house. She acted personally offended. Without saying so, she made him feel that he was not the man she had thought.

"It is only a bone," he had said.

"It is part of a human being," she had replied.

Thinking that a shadow had passed overhead, Malcolm looked up and saw two big birds circling. Vultures had found the carcass. Wouldn't vultures be a signal to anyone looking for the body? He wished Abdu would come.

He left the box of plums and took another armful of dry twigs over to the body and stood there holding them, looking down into a face now stiff and ugly. The horror of finding this corpse came down on him like an illness. Now the innocent were afraid. And now they really were responsible for something. What they did and didn't do would alter life forever for someone. It was not right, he was sure it was not right to burn him without knowing his name, without making it possible for his family to know that he was dead. He threw down the trash and, with a glance over his shoulder, squatted and began searching the soldier's pockets. The smell was getting stronger in the heat, and he wished he could hold his breath. He found a few coins in a front pocket and rolled the body partway to reach the hip pocket, where he found a small wallet. Inside were some tattered papers and a plasticized card. Quickly he stuffed these into his own hip pocket and put the wallet under the body.

On the terrace below, he found a rotten log, and managed to drag it up and tilt it across the dead boy's chest.

After an age, Abdu arrived with a cardboard box on his shoulder. In the box he had kindling wood, kerosene and matches, even a small hatchet. "I heard," he said, "that we found a dead dog." He seemed pleased.

Malcolm looked away quickly, realizing suddenly that he had insulted a man by calling him a dog. He intended to give him dignity again by rescuing his name from destruction, but his friend must not know.

He said, "Look," pointing at the vultures.

"I saw them. They will go away soon."

While Malcolm watched, Abdu doused everything with kerosene, the clothes, the skin, the hair, such hair as there was. Those kids were all practically skinned. Then he went to work, slicing the log expertly with the hatchet, placing each piece of wood, according to design, using the twigs and brush that Malcolm had piled up.

"When I make charcoal," he said, "I build a pyramid of wood, and it burns for two days. We want this to burn quickly and very hot." His hands might have been shaking slightly.

Malcolm said, "Too bad, you know; he was just a boy."

"It's too late for pity."

"Sure." He tried to keep his voice casual. "I was just thinking that he must have a family. I was wondering what you would want someone else to do, if Waleed or Hanni were lying dead in enemy territory."

Abdu got still for a moment, squatting on his heel, and then went back to work without looking at him. "I can tell you what would happen if Waleed or Hanni were lying dead in our brother's field."

It was a habit people had formed, to call the occupiers "brothers". The word implied bitterly the lack of choices left to the Lebanese ("We choose our friends.").

"They would take the watch from his arm, the money from his pocket, the shoes from his feet, the gold from his teeth, and then they would throw him to the coyotes. He would be eaten by the beasts. And no one would tell me he was dead."

"You would never know?"

"I could guess."

"My wife's brother was lost in Vietnam. He was never reported dead, but he never came home."

"That's the way war is."

"But it's very cruel. It killed his father slowly. My wife has never recovered, not really."

Abdu poured kerosene on the wood he had piled over the body. Then he carried the can nearly to the other end of the small orchard and set it down. Coming back, he took a little box of matches from his pocket, struck one and tossed it into the pile, which exploded into flames. Until the instant he did it, Malcolm hoped he wouldn't. The two of them jumped backward and stood staring at the fire, feeling the heat on their faces, the harsh kerosene smoke in their lungs.

Without taking his gaze from the fire, Abdu said, "*Ustaz*, I want to ask you. How can a man do what's right and the world the way it is?"

Flames were searing the limbs of two plum trees. The leaves were curling, the fruit peel frying and bursting. The smell of death was already replaced by other smells—fire, scorched fruit, burned cloth.

Malcolm said, "Maybe we should have moved him farther away."

Abdu said, "*Ma'leish*. Never mind," with profound resignation.

Malcolm was aware he had not answered a question, but he did not know what to say. He felt a subtle pressure in the area of his hip pocket, wondering what it was exactly that he had hidden there and how he would use it. Maybe it would offer a way to cleanse himself.

They stood there, friends and strangers, caught together in a trap, but he plotted to escape alone. The thought made him feel soiled and worried. He did not want to betray this good man, his favorite neighbor.

He said, "How long does it take a body to burn?"

"I don't know. I have never done this before."

"Do they send patrols down this road?"

"Never. They're scared."

They went back to picking plums, which were purple and smooth and firm. Occasionally they ate one. They filled most of the boxes they had brought with them. The orchard was full of wood smoke, an odor of kerosene and the stink of burning hair and flesh. The first black smoke dissipated, and a gray haze floated up the hillside, obscuring a vineyard, rising through the pine trees toward the fields and houses of the village. Everyone would know they had built a fire.

"Be careful what you say about this," Abdu told him. "They have agents everywhere."

"Even in the village?"

"Even in the village. Some of them we know. But there must be others. And careless people who talk."

Malcolm kept picking plums, slowly, but Abdu seemed to read his thoughts. He said, "Remember, *Ustaz*, what kind of people we are dealing with. You know that boy from the Abu Joudeh family? He's in prison because they didn't like his haircut.

"Yes. He was driving with a girl. The soldier at a checkpoint said, 'That's a very short haircut,' and the kid, he was just a dumb eighteen-year-old, said, 'It's a marine cut.' And the soldiers took him, car and all. They put the girl out on the road. For six months no one knew where the boy was. Finally, the parents paid an officer a big bribe for the information that he's in a certain prison in Damascus. A haircut, *Ustaz*! If a marine haircut means you're a marine, what about a body on my land?"

They heaved boxes of fruit into the car. When the fire began to smolder they added more fuel, and there was a new billow of black smoke. The sun was straight overhead, and Malcolm was soaked with sweat and exhausted. He drank too much water and accused Abdu of being part camel, because he was not thirsty.

When they sat down to rest, Abdu seemed satisfied. Hugging his big, bony knees, he said, "Without doubt, he was a Muslim. That shouldn't make it any better, I know, but it does, because I can't imagine them. Christians in any country are my brothers. Real brothers. They go to church and pray for their sons. Muslims, I don't know. They care, I'm sure, but I can't feel with them."

Malcolm was surprised by this frankness and, though he liked it and though he wanted to protest, he did not think of anything solid on which to hang an argument. Instead he asked, "What will their army do, if they keep losing men like this?"

"Probably they'll hit us really good."

They sat for a while, imagining that.

Finally Abdu said, "Your wife will be expecting you for lunch. Right?"

"Yes. She probably expected me before now."

"*Yalla*. Go then."

"I don't like leaving you before this is finished."

"*Ma'leish*, it might take a long time. Leave the boxes in the car until I come. I'll help you unload them. Except the one in the seat, near the left door. I chose those for Emily."

"It's more than we can eat."

"They will keep a long time. Just don't tell your wife how hard I made you work for them."

Malcolm looked up at Abdu to be sure he had understood the message. "Don't worry. Emily will never know."

Abdu walked to the car with him. "Be careful at the roadblock."

"They never bother me. I'm just a dumb foreigner."

Their eyes met and held, and Malcolm saw both weariness and its acceptance in the eyes of his friend. He started to turn away, but Abdu held out a hand to stop him and said, "You are a good man, *Ustaz*, and I love you very much. My sons love you. They always tell me that."

"Thank you. You are our best friends in the village."

"I'm depending on you, *Ustaz*, to keep our secret." His hand gripping Malcolm's was dry and callused and powerful.

"Of course," he said, already opening the car door and already feeling like a traitor. Why had he taken the soldier's papers except that he meant to tell someone?

When he got into the car, his feet felt slow, the steering wheel rigid. He wished he could stop somewhere and think before going home. The decision he had to make seemed to get more complicated by the moment, and, preoccupied with it, he forgot to think at all about the checkpoint. He was almost there when he remembered the papers in his hip pocket. It was too late to hide them. And suddenly he noticed that his hands were scratched and bloody from pulling on the thorns, though why it should matter, he didn't know.

The soldier took a long look at him, the same as the other one had when he came in the morning. Malcolm tried to look back at him calmly, tried to notice things like the man's careless uniform, his blue eyes and sunburned face, his rifle hanging casually over his shoulder. Beside him in the road another soldier stood with his rifle ready. He

had a groggy look and had not shaved for two or three days. The two
of them stared at him, one moving his hands on the rifle, deliberately.
There was no traffic. Only Malcolm.

"Where you come from?" the blue-eyed soldier said, in English.

"From my friend's orchard."

"Where you go?"

"To my house in the village."

"Passport," holding out his hand.

Malcolm leaned and took his passport from the pocket in the
dash. The soldier stared at the information in the front. He looked
at Malcolm and back at his picture. Then he turned a page and stared
at his visas, his entrance and exit stamps. The woods were very quiet.
Three hundred yards away, on the main road, a truck backfired. The
soldier with the rifle ready flinched and fidgeted. The car was like an
oven.

"What you do here?"

"I'm a teacher."

"Out," he said, tossing his head to demonstrate, and the other
supported the command with a motion of his rifle. Malcolm got out,
feeling sweat trickling from his armpits.

The soldier took him to the rear of the car and made a motion
like lifting the trunk lid, and Malcolm knew that he had to go back
for the key. His knees were shaking. He had to turn his back on the
soldier, and then was horrified to realize that he had put his hand to
his hip pocket and pushed down on the contents.

They lifted the trunk lid and looked at the boxes of plums and
into the small space behind them. The second soldier, meanwhile, got
into the front seat and rummaged through the pocket, then got out,
opened the rear door and stuck his head in. When he emerged, he had
four or five plums in his hands.

"*Ruuh*," they told him. "Go."

Malcolm fumbled the keys into the ignition and managed to
leave. His heart felt like an animal throwing itself against the bars of
a cage, and his face was burning from the heat of his fear. Thank God,
he thought. He wished he could laugh, but it was too soon. He

thought he would enjoy telling Abdu that they were stupid men at that checkpoint, but he could not tell Abdu why he was afraid. And on second thought, he was the first one who had been stupid.

Getting ready to shower before lunch, he locked the bathroom door. He never did that. His clothes smelled like fire. His hands trembled when he pulled the papers out of his pocket and put them on the counter beside the sink. A soldier's "personal effects", things that were sent to families when men died far from home. Though he could read Arabic a little, the scribbling on the scraps of paper was difficult. One paper was a form of some kind. With patience he would be able to figure it out. The plasticized card was an identification document. It had the soldier's name, his mother's name, his religion, the place and date of his birth.

As soon as he read it he knew that Abdu had been right. It was a mistake to know these things. There was no way to find a family in a big city with so little information, no way anyone could try without bringing suspicion on himself. And now there was no way to forget this name.

He tore the papers into tiny pieces and dropped them into the wastebasket, under some of Emily's tissues.

The card was thick and stiff, and he did not know yet what to do with it. Obviously he couldn't carry it around, and he couldn't let Emily find it. Maybe he could hide it in one of his books. She never read his economics books. But she did pick them up and clean the edges.

After his shower, when he started to put on his slippers, he noticed that the inside lining of the left one was loose, and on an impulse he slipped the card under the lining. Then he took the slipper to his desk and glued the lining back in place. The slippers were very old. One day when he was burning trash, he would throw them in.

He went downstairs and kissed Emily without looking at her. She said, "Did you have a good time?"

"We worked hard," he said, hoping she was not listening closely.

"What was burning down there?"

This casual questioning felt like having his pockets searched, but he managed to tell himself that it wasn't her fault. "We made a fire. We found a dead dog and burned him with a bunch of brush and junk." Something a lot worse than bringing home a thighbone, he added to himself.

"Good grief! You poisoned the whole village to get rid of a dead dog." She said it with good humor, while pouring steaming vegetables into a bowl.

He was pondering Abdu's question which he had never answered. Can a man do what's right?

She said, "The plums are beautiful, but as usual Abdu gave us too many."

"Make jam. Share them with someone." He heard the tonelessness, the indifference in his own voice. He was thinking that maybe someday, given time to put it all together, he could help her understand about her brother. But probably not.

All the while, she was saying something about their not being the right plums for jam and telling him he looked exhausted.

He sat at the table, facing the window. Smoke still covered the lower part of the hill, and the whole world smelled like burned flesh. Or maybe it smelled that way only to those who knew. Abdu must be sitting there, staring at the fire, waiting for the bones to become ashes, thinking that he had fallen into the hands of his foolish American friend and must trust him, because he had no alternative. Malcolm felt then that a lock snapped shut inside of him, and he visualized a chain, running down the hill, dropping over terrace walls, lying in the dark soil of vegetable patches, sliding around tree trunks, linking him to the man who sat by the fire. He would never escape this chain; it could stretch to the ends of the earth without breaking. Nor would he have peace. But he would be a friend. He would protect Abdu's sons. And he would never burden this good man with the truth that it was a Christian boy from Aleppo whom they burned in the orchard.

He remembered a silly thing that kids in his high school used to say when they had offended someone. "Excuse me for living," they said. Like a lot of silly things, it was almost right. Being alive, one had to ask forgiveness.

A House on the Beach

I go to Hamra St without a shopping list and walk up and down, looking for something. The shop windows are opulent with gold and leather, the overhanging balconies streaked with rust. I stop to stare at fashions so new they might be from another planet. Or is it my face in the glass, my empty expression which is out of place? I consider buying half a kilo of chocolates. Instead I join one of the two streams flowing in opposite directions on the sidewalk, each pushed or drawn by the movement of the other, without touching. I observe that with the passage of time the small trees along the curb are leafing and growing, becoming more identical, while the people on the streets are digressing and evolving, becoming more distinct and dissimilar, strangers, perhaps, even to one another.

Just ahead on the corner people are chattering at tables in an outdoor café. The smell of their coffee reaches me in whiffs. Cars beep, a stringed instrument and a male voice wail, and a vendor shouts, "*Ah sakkiin, ya batiix!*"

The other sound is already a memory before I grasp it—a thin singing whistle and a bang, followed by fainter whistles and bangs, garbled like echoes. Someone bumps me, hurrying past, a metal shutter screeches and clangs, and when I turn the street is almost empty. The few remaining people are ducking into doorways, cars are running red lights and turning down alleys, and I am frozen on the walk behind a guardrail, there to keep me from stepping off the curb. I stand beside it paralyzed and look up the street, which is still now and waiting, while the love song plays on. Around the corner the faces of buildings are cluttered with jutting signs, at different heights, in various sizes, naming doctors, shoe-repair shops, money-changers and Hammaoui's Art School. Between them a small gap beckons to me.

In the narrow place between plastered walls, all is dark except for two rays of sun slanting in like searchlights, and a young man in a white shirt joins me there, diving into the space just as bullets spatter in the street. There are sharp explosions like hand grenades, and I imagine a shell dropping through the opening and exploding into hot flying razors. My body shakes as though I am standing in an icy rain.

And then it is over. I stay in my shelter until a service taxi goes by honking, looking for a fare, and a woman starts sweeping her broken window off the sidewalk. Then I come out and walk to the corner, and the tables of the sidewalk café are full again and waiters in red jackets bustle about. I ask anxious questions, and everyone assures me, "There is nothing."

A yellow garbage truck rumbles by. People are ordering lemonade and telling me, "Don't be afraid." In the middle of the block someone is throwing a bucket of water on a red spot in the street, and I walk carefully, with my legs trembling, watching pink water run into the gutter.

Once when I was a child my mother threw a pail of dirty water out the back door, just as I ran past. Suddenly I was strangling, drenched, filthy—an ambushed four-year-old. The aftermath was wonderful. She bathed me, held me, rubbed my hair dry, apologized, kissed me. And laughed. We still laugh when we remember.

Didn't someone try to tell me that I would be lonely here?

"Tell me about these people. How did you know them?"

"I was somewhere by the sea, on a little stretch of beach, shrouded in fog. The sea was black. Black and white waves were heaving up onto the shore, and spray was flying in my face. I was trudging through the sand in tennis shoes. The sand was soft and mushy and sucked at my feet. I kept leaning forward, trying to hurry.

"Everything was drifting, vague. Then I saw a man and woman walking together in front of me. They were definite, substantial figures against the swirling fog, as clear and focused as models in a magazine. The breeze lifted a corner of his handsome coat and played with the hem of her skirt. Their elegance was undisturbed. I leaned and stumbled in the sand, but they were erect and poised. Their grace made me feel awkward and foolish."

"Can you describe their faces?"

I couldn't, though I knew they were beautiful and young and in love. His arm circled her waist, casually, suggesting possession rather than desire. When she spoke to him he bent his head so that the words rose from her lips into his ear instead of being snatched by the wind. Without quite hearing it, I recognized the warmth and energy of Arabic. Courtesy, I thought, required me to drop farther back, but I felt desperate to hurry on, to escape this sand, to get to someplace where I was going.

The couple felt me there behind them and turned together, glancing over their shoulders to see me. They smiled. They said, "*Bonjour*, madame. *Ahlan wa sahlan.*" Their eyes were wide and dark as the sea.

We walked together. They spoke to me in my own language, their consonants tight and precise. "Do you like this country? Have you seen the cedars? The caves? You are welcome, madame." Companionship loosed my feet, so that I walked with slow, easy steps like theirs.

A house emerged then, out of the mist, an old Lebanese house of thick stones with arched windows, tall and narrow. The mellow colors of the stones gave off a gentle light, and tiles rippled, faded red, along the edge of the roof.

"Bring your family to the beach and take a vacation," the man told me. "A vacation is what you need."

"Yes, and there is no better place than here," she said. Then, on an impulse natural as breathing, she lifted a graceful hand toward the old mansion and added, "Why don't you use our house?"

Awed into silence, I heard them boast that the house was spacious and well-equipped. "And we will be away all month."

Against my protest, the young man said, "You must. We insist, because it will make us happy."

"It will make us happy," they said together.

After battles I do things like this, trying to get on with my life, sometimes not remembering why I must. At the wheel of my car, I bump and twist my way through a shattered city. The roads are lined with vehicles, burned in their parking places. Poles lean, webs of wire wrap the front of a broken building. A mangled bicycle teeters on the edge of a balcony, high above the sidewalk, and the fallen railing blocks the street. Other people are in their cars, fighting the obstacles, too, so many that an exhausted and angry soldier stands in an intersection, forcing us to wait for one another. All the tires crunch over spent bullets and broken concrete.

Near the benzene station, black and twisted, a man has fallen backward in the street, his arms thrown out, and lies in a puddle resembling dried tar. Everybody is driving around him: an ambulance, families with mattresses on the car, people going back to work, sightseers, and I. Slowly I pass, looking at the body. He is a big man, wearing ridiculous green pants. One of his shoes lies a few yards away. I look for his wound and find a clotted hole in his knit shirt, in his side.

At the corner a salesman with a week-old beard and hopeful eyes offers crystal from a cloth laid out on the curb, extending it toward frustrated drivers and pedestrians who seem startled, as though they have just emerged from shelters into too much light. They rush around purposefully (looking for food, water, someone who is lost?). All of us are like ants, running to and fro through a smashed nest. We know the way. These ruins are already ancient.

The house was so large we didn't need it all. We unpacked small suitcases, expressing to one another our amazement that we had a house on the beach, not one of those bare little cabins or cramped apartments but a villa, decorated and furnished like a fine hotel.

In the light of morning, I lay on the bed listening to the soft pulsing of the sea, sensing from its sound that the wind and fog had gone, that the sun was warming the pale sand and glittering off the ruffled surface of blue water. I could see a long stretch of shoreline without even leaving the bedroom, without getting up. I was content there, studying the elaborate designs in the carpet and the carved frame around the mirror. I could see my husband walking on the beach and know his pleasure in the clean air, though I was lying there, staring at the glass chandelier in the middle of the ceiling.

One of the children began to explore the house. She opened the door to a bedroom we had not used the night before. I could see her down the hall, a short, sturdy child with filtered sunlight behind her, holding the door open, staring into the room.

"Mother," she said, "there is a dead man in this room."

There was a flatness in her voice, making the statement an observation only, like the opposite equivalent of "Mother, there is an empty bed in this room."

And in the same way that I saw the blue of the water and my husband relaxing as he walked, I could see the body on the bed, dressed in dark trousers and a white shirt, a pale, puffy, middle-aged face with a mustache and a small black spot on the left temple. He lay staring at the ceiling. He could be alive except that he did not move.

"Never mind," I heard myself saying. "Just shut the door."

He had been here all along, I thought, and then let my image of him float backward through time to see him staring at the ceiling while we slept, lying motionless while we moved in and unpacked our clothes.

The child closed the door.

"It is none of our business," I told her. "Go out and play."

She went. She ran down the hill and along the beach to catch up with her father. The sun sprayed off the prisms of the chandelier in red moving lines. The sea breathed in and out peacefully.

Two processions pass through a city street, while I look down from a balcony. Blaring horns accompany the first. A string of jeeps, station wagons, small trucks, old cars race past shuttered shops and scarred facades—blowing, beeping, screaming. The middle car drags an object, tied to its bumper. Debris sloughs off the object as it bounces and scrapes against the concrete, some of it smearing the road, bits of it sticking to the windshield of the car behind. The image of this strange object burns into my eyeballs to remain, unidentified, until I see my neighbor's face, as she turns away nauseous, and I close my eyes to find it again. A wave of heat passes through my body. The dragging blob is flesh, a diminishing piece of a human being, tied by the ankles to a speeding car.

The second procession passes silently, except for footfalls, a multitude of footfalls, irregular, shuffling, weary, dreadful. The sound of these many footfalls grows and swells, as the parade nears, until it rumbles like an approaching earthquake. I look down on a mass of silent people, wearing black in the summer sun. They look like dead people, whose feet move without their knowledge. Seven caskets, seven fresh wooden boxes ride on the shoulders of the crowd, ride lightly as though they are empty. Knowledge sweeps across the city and reaches even me: these are seven young men hit by one shell. May they rest in peace. Bronze censers swing from the hands of silent priests. Behind each casket mourners trudge, forming a procession within the procession. Their bowed heads and bent shoulders indicate an invisible load, but the caskets are buoyant, alive. A young soldier, as though suddenly waking, lifts his arms and cries out, "Me too, God; let me go with them."

I think about the gracious custom of escorting as far as possible a visitor who is departing. An impulse flickers in me, a need—to join the mourners, to wear black, to be grieved.

When again our daughter opened the door of the extra room and looked inside, she was no longer a child but a young lady taller than I. She was startled and indignant. Apparently she didn't remember what happened yesterday when she was a little girl.

"Mother," she said, "there is a dead man in this room."

I felt wearied that she had mentioned the matter again, and this time not as mere observation. There was intimidation in her voice, an accusation that something was wrong.

The accusation required the defensiveness in my reply. "It is not my concern."

"But, Mother, he has a bullet hole in his head."

Again I saw the body, lying stiffly with the arms straight, and the eyes open, and black, dried blood on the pale temple.

"Look," I told her. "This is not our house, and he was here when we came. Just shut the door."

She shut the door. She looked at me and sighed.

I remembered the elegance of the couple strolling on the beach, their kindness in reaching out to me.

"If we tell anyone," I argued, "we may offend the nice people who invited us here."

The traffic slows here by the benzene station, because of the body partially blocking the street. This man has been dead so long he is huge and black like the carcass of a cow in a field. Doesn't he belong to someone? I have driven around him morning and evening for so many days. Each time his belly is bloated more, stretching those silly green pants. I try not to look anymore, because I am embarrassed for him that his torn and stinking body is exposed to public view.

Today the smelly yellow truck stops, and two men leap off at the back. They have shovels in their hands. The rear of the truck opens, a panel falling down to become a scoop. This reveals in the yawning belly of the truck a heap of refuse with arms and legs protruding here and there. The men push their shovels under the body. Together they lift their load onto the scoop, which begins to rise and fold in. The truck swallows, with a churning noise.

They have left the black puddle and the shoe.

I drive on, troubled by the suspicion that I have forgotten or lost something.

"When did you discover the body in the house?"

I was sitting on a slatted bench in a room as lonely as a desert. The floor was speckled with spit and grime, and the walls were dirty yellow, smudged by shoe heels and grubby hands. Behind the desk one picture hung crookedly, the face in the frame familiar and troubling. Stacks of paper files with ragged edges covered the tables and the floors.

A man with a bitter face was asking me questions. Sometimes he was wearing a uniform, at other times a gray suit. There was something disappointed and sad about him, but relentless. He wrote on his forms and talked to me dryly, without looking up. I felt cornered, realizing he thought it strange that I had come now and not before. Why did you not report it immediately? This was the question looming before us. I found it fascinating in itself, like a curio from a far country. Why did I not? When I turned it over in my mind all the meaning spilled out quickly, like sand from a pail. I did not know why, only that I was falling into some mysterious trouble.

He saved this question, perhaps to catch me with it at the end. It took the shape of a metal trap with jagged teeth and lay on the desk near his elbow, while he questioned me about little details: the layout of the rooms, how many keys there were. He made me draw a map and mark the spot where the body lay. Then he didn't like what I drew. He claimed it contradicted things I had said before. I grew weary, and my weariness was stitched with anger. Who was this man dead in our vacation house that I should have to answer questions? Why did he keep intruding on my life?

My interrogator asked again about my relationship to the house and its owners, and I related things as I remembered them.

"I was driving, in a dimness like twilight, on a road overhung with the long, limp leaves of eucalyptus trees. Ahead of me a line of traffic stopped. There was a roadblock, a checkpoint for soldiers or vigilantes or outlaws. Looking past the line of cars and trucks, I saw people at the barrier, carrying big rifles in their hands and wearing hoods over their heads. They were like the pictures in the papers of hooded men prowling the streets with guns, only they were not pictures, but an awesome presence. They waited by the twisted circles of barbed wire. The vehicles in front of me began to slide sideways, slipping off the road slowly, as though repelled by the faceless men.

They opened a great space in front of me. I could go back by shifting into reverse; it was not too late. But I began to drive straight ahead, compelled by some perverse fascination. I wanted to go back, but I could not make myself. I could not move my foot to put it on the brake. The group of people with rifles ready, looking at me through little slits in their hoods, came closer, growing larger and larger and filling up my windshield."

"You were kidnapped?" he said.

"Kidnapped?" Suddenly I could remember nothing but the elegant couple on the beach, and I said, "No. I was invited."

"By people wearing masks?"

Astonishing thought. I could not answer this question.

"What is their name? Where did they go? Why have they not returned?" he asked, already knowing that I had no answers to these questions.

"Look, I came voluntarily. I'm trying to help you."

"And you think that because you walked in, you can turn and walk out?"

Another uniformed man arrived, dragging a very old man, dressed only in underwear. The captive whined and babbled and tried to kiss the hand of the man behind the desk, but he could not. His wrists were tied behind him with a rope. They were bleeding. The interrogator looked at him with disdain and by a flick of his eyelids announced his fate. As the policeman dragged the old man away, he cried, "No, no," like a terrified child. My limbs began to shiver.

Then a woman entered, caution in her movements, placed some papers on the desk and took a step backward. The officer glanced down at the papers without touching them and shouted, "These are rubbish! Useless!" The woman fled.

He looked at me again and said, "You are hiding something."

"No, sir, your honor."

A hint of a smile, cynical and proud, touched his lips. "What were you doing in that house?"

"I wanted to belong, to be a part of... life. Then everything went wrong."

"So why didn't you do something about the body?"

"It was like a dream that needed an explanation."

"No, it was an explanation that you didn't understand."

"I didn't know anything. I was only passing by, and everybody went around him, not just me. He was part of the debris—a gutted building, some toppled poles, a burned car, a dead human."

"You don't seem to understand. There has been a murder."

"He was obscene; he smelled bad. His belly kept stretching more and more. He lost a shoe. His socks were black. What else do you want to know?"

"The extent of your role. That's all. And I will find out. The information is here in these files." The shabby folders had multiplied and were everywhere—under the desk, leaning against the walls. They were covered with Arabic scribbling and little brown circles left by coffee cups. He laid his hand on one at the corner of the desk, and I saw my name stamped on it in black ink. "But it will go better for you if you talk."

I crossed my legs, trying to hide the shaking. "The body was there when I arrived. Stiff, shot in the head."

"Are you accusing someone? That also would be to your advantage."

I am their guest.

As though he heard my thought, he said, "Or accomplice?"

They were so kind. There on the beach in the fog, they had said, "It will make us happy." What happened to them?

"You were running away. Now they have run away."

Could they have tricked me? "I was not running. I was a bystander."

His voice whipped at me. "There are no bystanders anymore. It has been forbidden."

He gave me time to be shaken by that. Then he said, "What about him? Who is he?"

He? Oh, the dead man. "It's not my business. I am a visitor. That's what it says on my passport."

He held out his hand then, as though to take the evidence that would support me, and hope leaped up in my breast, but as I began to search, my bag became huge and awkward. I fumbled at buckles. I groped through chaotic contents. Each document appeared to be the one, then, in a kind of fluid deterioration, became meaningless paper. My interrogator waited. Beyond the yellow wall the sound of gunfire grew, a sharp and urgent sound. The blood sank through my limbs, leaving my body empty. "I have it," I said, my voice only a whisper, "I know I have it," tearing the lining out of the bag, ripping the pockets from my coat.

"You are deceived," he said. "Your identity means nothing."

The opening of the door is like an explosion splitting the air in front of my face. Or maybe an actual explosion has blown the door in. My breath stops. The sun slants in viciously, and I cannot move a hand to protect my eyes. Part of me has died in the night. Down in the street bullets crackle, as in my dream. I can almost remember it, something about being arrested, nearly naked. Or nearly transparent. I was in big trouble; I had done something wrong. Gauzy white curtains stir softly, and I know this is my bedroom. My pretty pink bedroom on a battlefield... My mouth tastes like something dead. The battle has come to us. And though my heart is beating again, I cannot move or cry out. My arms are numb. Sorrow sits like a stone on my chest.

I can hear my neighbors running toward the basement. A pounding at the door. "Come down, madame. Hurry, come down."

I cannot hurry. I am overcome with inertia, as though I have arrived after a long journey. Slowly, slowly I perceive that all is well. We are in this trouble together.

Moonrise

I dreamed I swallowed a scorpion. In an agony of thirst I reached for the bottle, pale-green and sweating, with a drop of water sliding down its slope, and when I lifted it, I saw tiny bubbles rising through the liquid and bursting like sparks in the mouth of the bottle. The drink was sweet and cold on my tongue, and then it was fire in my throat. The small beast—feelers and forked feet and stingers—settled slowly to the bottom of the bottle, even while I knew that I had already swallowed him.

I woke to the sound of gunfire. My abdomen was swollen tight under the bandage, and the scorpion clawed at my throat. When I moved, everything hurt. Like part of the pain, a feeling lurked in the edges of my waking, a feeling of anticipation or dread, and I didn't know yet if it was valid or just a memory from my dream.

Beyond my window a pink light glowed, outlining a long row of startling figures on the outside ledge, their shapes like fists raised, spears pointed, heads in grotesque wigs and helmets and feathers. As I stared, everything grew in intensity—the pink light, the gunfire, and the black shadows on the window ledge.

The waiting feeling evolved into knowledge. This was the day when the doctor would bring the lab report. And Amineh would come. The oppositeness of these two expectations fascinated me for a moment. One small hope subtracted, one small emptiness filled.

Strings of shots like firecrackers, interspersed with big explosions like rockets, broke through my distraction. There was a battle somewhere in the streets.

Stretching to reach my tiny radio and lifting it from the bedside table stirred up a barrage of pains in my side and restored the ache in the back of my bruised left hand, the only part of me still attached to a tube. And I saw the green bottle, dry now, half-empty, evidence that I had drunk something besides anise tea. Not everything had been a dream. The head nurse, who always feigned astonishment that I had not eaten my food, would, I thought, treat that bottle like a suicide weapon. She was right, almost. The fizzy drink I longed for had hurt like crazy, made everything worse.

The Voice of Lebanon was playing soothing music. Pianos and strings. A breath of emotion in it, a glimmer of candlelight. Outside, the crackle of rifles. A grenade exploding. I listened a long time, with the little radio in my lap, and there was nothing but music. Bad news, I thought. It's always bad news when they leave us to figure things out for ourselves.

The music faded and was replaced by a sweet female voice, whispery, intimate. "Good morning, to every one of you, wherever you are, and God's blessings upon you this day. Especially to all Lebanese, at home or abroad. We love you. We wish you health and safety and love."

After the sugary editorial, more strings and pianos. The shadows on the windowsill dissolved, just as I remembered that they were only my plants, and day advanced into the room. Machine guns joined the battle. The scorpion clawed.

The doctor would be in a hurry. We used to have so many doctors; we thought they made up excuses to cut us open. Now that we need them, we have so few, always in a hurry. He would be cheerful, though, whether it seemed appropriate or not. He would tell me what everyone already knew (I made him promise), and his words would sting like the scorpion. Then Amineh, young and fragile friend, would come and sit by my bed.

For sure it was the day, if this was Thursday. Other days she graded papers or shopped for her mother or prepared dinner. On Thursday afternoons we usually had our classes. I taught her things from the Bible, and she taught me French. The week might resemble a turbulent sea, but Thursday afternoon floated in it, like an island of peace and purpose. We studied. We prepared, in case there would be tomorrow.

The cleaning woman was about the age of my Susie. Her face bore the expression of a child expecting to be struck in a moment, yet her arrival was like an attack. She brought in the biting smells of soap and disinfectants. She jerked open the curtain, letting sunshine pounce onto my blanket. She made a lot of noise with the bucket of water and the wastebaskets and the mop handle against door facings. When she banged the corner of my bed with a chair, I winced.

"Sorry," she said.

She was wearing a limp blue uniform and a scarf tied under her hair. Her skin was young and smooth, her arms round, her hands soft, plump. She scrubbed the floor. When the guns clattered, she clicked her tongue.

"Listen to them," she said, "killing each other. Crazy people. Crazy." Her voice was a little too loud, a little too shrill.

"Who's shooting?" I asked her.

She looked at me startled, stood up, gestured. "Our men. It's all our own men, shooting each other, throwing bullets and bombs on our own houses. Crazy people. Crazy Lebanese people."

"What happened?"

"What happened? What do I know?" She took both hands off the mop to open them in helplessness. "Our street was full of people last night, and shells started to fall. I grabbed my little brother by the shirt. Otherwise, the second shell would have killed him. Our neighbor lost her boy."

She was mopping again, expressing rage in the violence of her movements. "They argued," she said. "The forces are divided now, fighting each other. The same enemy, but they disagree on how to win, or probably on who's in control. So they fight. Crazy people. They will destroy us."

"Weren't you afraid to come to work?"

"Of course I was afraid," she said, "but I was more afraid not to come to work."

For a while she mopped and muttered. "Ten lira for a kilo of potatoes. Three or four potatoes. Rotten in the middle."

She straightened up to look at me. "I'm afraid of bullets, but I'm more afraid my family will starve. Who's going to do anything if I don't?"

I kept asking questions and she kept explaining in angry, jerking sentences. Her family were refugees from the south. Her father had been wounded and was crippled, permanently in bed, she the oldest child, the only one old enough to work. A variation on a dominant theme: the pain of a country at war with itself.

She rearranged the furniture, her plastic shoes flopping on the wet floor. I imagined my Susie in those shoes, scrubbing floors for a living, her intelligence outraged. And Amineh with her small hands, her fear of not becoming anybody.

She picked up the wastebasket and carried it out into the hall. When she came back I said, "Will you do one more thing for me?"

"What's that?"

"Bring my flowers inside."

"Of course," she said, with her back to me.

She arranged them in a colorful bank along the inside ledge, put a small one on my tray table and still had several big baskets for the floor. And now they were flowers again, tulips and jonquils, mums and violets and roses and a green plant with long pointed leaves. All gifts from my friends. The room was bright and warm from their presence.

She had left the window open a crack, and the gunfire was louder, loud enough to be in the street beside the hospital. But I knew that gunfire always sounds closer than it really is. She picked up her pail and her mop and went out muttering, "Crazy people." The room smelled fresh and clean.

Beyond the gray, flat roofs of Dowra and Bourj Hammoud, the mountain loomed, as clean and bright as my room, covered with towns. I knew that if I could stand at the window, I would see the smooth blue bay and ships and the bridge crossing over the road from Sin el Fil and joining Ashrafiyeh to the *autostrad* north. Instead I was looking through golden air, ignorant of what was happening down in the streets.

When it was time for news we were told that negotiations were under way to solve a misunderstanding. We were asked to believe that there were no fundamental differences between the leaders of the forces but "certain people" had tried to sow discord for their own personal gain. These people would not succeed in destroying the unity of the people. Etc., etc. for fifteen minutes, without saying where the fighting was, what the objectives might be or anything about casualties. The last time this happened, I remembered, boys in our town killed people they had gone to school with.

How I longed for a cup of coffee, very hot and black. But when it was finally time for breakfast, I got a piece of bread, a little dish of *lebne* and a cup of anise tea, tepid anise tea. I actually like anise tea, very hot, at bedtime. It makes me sleepy almost instantly. When you've just lost part of your insides, it's bedtime all day long.

Imagining saying all this to Roger, I knew his answer. "You must be feeling better, Jenny; you've started to complain."

The bread and *lebne* tasted wonderful. I chewed carefully for a long time, and when I swallowed, it became a rock too big to go down. For a moment I felt sick. The pain sank lower and lower, as it did once when I was a child and swallowed a piece of ice. I drank a bit of the tea, which was not even tepid anymore. I dozed and when I woke, it was hours yet before anyone would come.

Finally, noticing that the shooting was getting worse, I realized that probably nobody would come at all. Roger would be too wise. I can always count on Roger to be sensible. And Amineh? Surely someone would stop her. I hoped someone would stop her, even though my spirits sank, imagining what it would be like to have darkness come again without seeing her.

I ran through dialogues telling her about a wonderful lab report. It was benign after all. I would live a hundred years. She would smile and say, "*Khayyy...?*" in that odd open-ended way she had of saying it, making her exclamation sound like a question.

I willed the doctor not to come. Until he came, I wouldn't know.

I didn't really know, did I? Did the thing removed have to be what it looked like? Couldn't a doctor be wrong?

He came late, but he came. I recognized his quick steps in the hall, and I used that last moment of not knowing to look around at my flowers. The tulips were stunning, red and white together. A gift from smiling, handsome Tony. The violets, delicate like the evening light on the mountains, were from Nadia, who tends them in little pots for giving away. The jonquils looked so fresh and glad. The pastor and his wife brought them, then held both my hands and prayed. Roger's roses. I tried to hold on to this moment, aware that until then, I had paid so little attention to what it means to be well.

He stood at the foot of the bed, with his hands in the pockets of his white coat, and said, "You had a type B malignancy, grade two. It could have been better. It could have been worse. Nothing in the lymph nodes. That's good."

Maybe for a moment my whole body stopped working, not just my heart and my breath. I tried to think of things I should ask, but my head was empty.

"Are you in pain?" he asked.

Even the pain had stopped, but I remembered that I had meant to complain. "Yes. My abdomen is about to pop, and I've got a burning in my throat."

He walked around the bed and lifted the sheet. While he poked my tummy, making me gasp, he said, "I'm turning your case over to an oncologist. He should be in to see you in a day or two."

The right question suddenly came to me. I said, "Is it going to come back?"

"Fifty per cent no. Fifty per cent yes. In five years, more or less. Half of those come in about a year, at the place where we put the colon back together. We can't tell. You'll have checkups. The oncologist will decide how often." He looked me in the eyes and said, "I don't usually speak so plainly with patients, but you said I had to."

"Thank you," I said. "I really appreciate it."

On his way out of the room he turned and said, "I'm going to send you some tablets. Suck them; they'll help the burning and get some of that gas up."

Having knocked me down, he was going to leave, and I would be alone with the news and a great tumult of gunfire nearby. I stopped him for a moment by saying, "Where's the fighting?"

"All over." He gestured with his arms. "Around the bridges, between here and Dowra, over on the square by the post office. I guess the worst is in Sin el Fil."

"Bad news."

He said, "Lebanon is very sick," and left. The emptiness of the room closed in around me.

Roger called. The sound of the phone was joy. "Did you sleep O.K.?" he asked me, his voice full of friendliness and optimism, as always.

"I had bad dreams. I think the drugs do that."

"Did the doc come in yet?"

So I told him the news.

"That's good," he said. "Boy, it could have been a lot worse. He'll give it to us in writing?"

I had not even thought of that.

He told me that he had gotten to the office without any trouble but it would be risky to go any farther down the hill. "I hear that the road is cut just this side of the river. Will you be O.K.?"

I told him I would be O.K.

"Can you hear gunfire?"

"Yes. It sounds close sometimes. The doctor told me they're fighting at the square by the post office."

"Oh yeah? You need anything?"

"Call Susie and Rick," I told him. "Tell them..."

"I'll try," he said. "You know how it is on a day like this. I feel lucky just to get through to the hospital. Anyway I'll tell them you're gonna lick this the way you always lick everything." And then, "I'm sorry, Jenny. It's a bad day not to be able to come. If this clears up maybe I can come in the late afternoon."

"I hope so," I told him.

"Bummer, Sweetie. I'm praying for you. Don't forget that."

When I got the receiver back on the hook, I was so tired I had to lie still and take a rest. A feeling of disappointment crept over me. The call was finished and there were things I had needed to say and did not identify soon enough. I should have told him to sleep in the shelter tonight. I needed to tell him that the part about percentages is very confusing, and it is a lonely business being sick, that no one is getting inside of it with me, that I might be devastated even if I am not afraid.

Rick will wish he could come home, I thought, but he has other responsibilities now. And Susie will not quite believe her daddy's version, not until she hears it from me. But she will not be able to call, and she will be alone with it, there in her new place and her new job, alone like me, like Lebanon. Because Lebanon is sick, the lines that reach her are broken, and she is alone. More than that, because Lebanon is broken, the pieces are alone, the roads closed, the bridges under attack.

A nurse came in. Everything about her was careless, the state of her hair, her walk, the way she wore her uniform. She handed me a sealed sheet of tablets that had apparently been removed from a larger package. "Dr. Naseef told me to give you these."

I wanted to ask her to help me go to the bathroom, but she was so casual I felt she was unofficial, like she was not a nurse at all but a stranger who happened along and was asked to deliver the medicine. I didn't want to offend her. Besides, I feared that she had not slept in a long time.

I fumbled with one of the little foil sections and got it open. The tablet was square and yellow-green, sweet and chalky. I ate two, one after the other, and they left a dirty feeling in my mouth, but they calmed the scorpion a little and eased the pressure in my stomach.

Fifty per cent no; fifty per cent yes. I tried to think what that really meant. Half the chances in a hundred, either way. Fifty no; fifty yes. Fifty don't; fifty do. Fifty live; fifty die. What does that mean when I am only one? A flip of the coin. One flip, not a hundred. And when it comes up heads, its one hundred per cent heads. It comes up tails, it's all tails. The beast is there, or he's not there.

I could be praying; I should be praying. I don't know why I'm not praying. Maybe when you're sick, all the lines go down, and the truth gets jammed inside yourself.

Somebody brought me anise tea. I asked her to take me to the bathroom. With one hand she held me and with the other my movable tower with the swinging plastic bag. When we made it back to the bed, I knew I had been on a long journey. The severed muscles in my abdomen quivered and made me cry out. The needle was torturing my bruised hand. I drank the tea to wash some of the chalk out of my mouth, then lay very still and dozed.

When I woke up I knew it was not even lunchtime. Not even time for that soup, the soup that tasted like the water they had washed a chicken in. And when the soup comes and I don't eat it, hours yet 'til Amineh comes. Dear Amineh, who is not coming anyway because they are shooting. Explosions are shaking the walls. The crazy people are killing each other. The sirens are crying.

The sun was high, lighting the face of the mountain, and a column of smoke was rising out of Dowra. I wondered, as I had so many times before when I saw battle smoke, if someone were dying under that dark column. Was he alone? And in pain? If I hurt, imagine what it means, I thought, to have your body torn open by shrapnel.

I couldn't eat the soup. I was starving, and I couldn't eat it. I couldn't pray. My tummy was bursting and the world exploding, and I couldn't pray. All I could do was sleep. In my sleep I was trying to read the words on a bottle. They kept slipping away, unrecognized. They broke into meaningless fragments. They boomed and echoed in my skull and escaped again. Those elusive shapes and syllables were the essential words I needed to know. I chased them and struggled with them. I pronounced them again and again without attaching them to any idea or image or action.

Her small hand was lying on my wrist, a touch as uncertain as a dream, and when I opened my eyes she was standing beside the bed, wearing some kind of white coat.

"Your limbs are jerking," she said.

Her face was more anxious than usual, but there was fight and boldness in her eyes.

"I'm surprised to see you."

"I had to come," she said. "Your arms and legs were jerking. The muscles in your face were twitching."

"I think I was having a bad dream."

"Why?"

Amineh always asks why, and I never know the why of anything. I said, "You forgot to say hello."

"Hello." She leaned and kissed both my cheeks and the first one again, like a proper Lebanese friend. "Did your doctor come? Did he bring the lab report?"

I wanted to avoid the question a little longer, but knowing she would make me tell her, I just plunged in and hurried through.

"It's good," I added at the end. "It could have been a lot worse." I heard myself mimicking Roger.

She stood there thinking about it, with her eyelids lowered.

"I'm sorry," she said, and I thought a muscle twitched in her cheek, ever so slightly.

"Please sit down."

She only glanced at the chair and said, "I can't stay long."

"How did you get here?"

"In the Red Cross ambulance. I'm working with a rescue squad today."

"I didn't know you ever did that."

"I don't usually, in fact never. Your voice is tired. Have you been talking a lot?"

"No, I've hardly talked at all. Then why today?"

"I knew we'd eventually get to Jeitawi Hospital."

I was so surprised I couldn't say anything, and she added, "I had to see you."

I tried to grasp the fact that she had been running around a battlefield.

"I got here. Finally." She looked a little sick.

"You brought somebody to the hospital?"

She nodded. "A guy with a hole in his chest. I saw his heart beating." She made a big circle with her fingers and said, "Through this hole, I saw it."

I felt so sad because of the hole in this stranger's chest. "Will he make it?"

"No."

"Sit down," I told her. "You need a little rest."

She sat down in the plastic visitor's chair and leaned her head against the high back. "I guess I'm not feeling O.K." After a moment she added, "Nadia does this kind of thing all the time. She must be tougher than I am."

We sat quietly for a moment, and then she said, "My mother's getting crazy."

"Because of what you're doing?"

She nodded. "And Dory is out there, too."

"Where?"

She shrugged. "The militia called him last night. He took his gun and left."

I was silent, feeling sympathetic with her mother. One son already crippled in this war, and the other one fighting.

"I really didn't want to stay in the house. I knew she would cry all day. It's useless to cry. Especially about things that didn't happen yet."

When I didn't answer, she lifted her head and said, "*Muzboot?*"

"Right. *Muzboot.*"

There was gunfire in the distance. The saddest sound in the world is gunfire in the distance.

She got up and went to the window. I could no longer see her face. Long dark hair curled on the shoulders of the white coat. The coat was too big for her. She said, "Remember my friends Ghassan and Latifeh? They're going to Africa. He thinks he can get a job there." And after a heavy silence, "You know Colette? She left two days ago, to France."

I couldn't think of anything to say.

She turned around and sat down again before she said, "I can't blame them. This is not a country anymore."

Her eyes closed, and when she closes her eyes all the audacity and strength leave her face. Her mouth became very soft and beautiful, the way it looks when she is going to cry. She didn't cry. Her eyes opened, bigger and darker, and she said, "It's O.K. When people leave, I just quit loving them."

We sat in silence for a while until she said, "Are you going to leave me, too?"

"I'm not planning to." And after a few seconds I added, "I can't take the consequences."

She thought for a long moment, and I could see she had decided to ignore that last part. I was glad, because I had meant it to be lighthearted and then it wasn't. She looked at me and said, "I'll get really mad if you lie to me."

"You should get mad if I lie to you."

She quit looking at me, looked at something on the bedside table and said, "Of course, there are things you can't control, I know."

I had started to feel very tired and to sense that the conversation was going to develop beyond my strength. I had to think carefully how to answer. Finally I said, "But we don't cry until they happen. *Muzboot?*"

She smiled for the first time. It made her whole face come alive. She said, "You caught me," and kept smiling. Then she was grave again suddenly. "You were so pale. I felt scared when I saw you sleeping."

"I must be always pale when I'm sleeping."

She looked from the flowers on the table to those in the window and said, "I should have brought you flowers."

I thought that seeing her was more beautiful than flowers, but I didn't know if I could say it without sounding silly. I said, "Why? Because I don't have any?"

We rested for a few moments, then her eyes flew open, and she said, "A siren is going to start down there, and I'll have to go. It's a signal."

"I'll be afraid, hearing shooting and knowing you're on the road."

She smiled without showing her pretty teeth, thinking about saying something, not sure. But I knew she would say whatever it was.

"When I was a kid, about sixteen, I used to carry a pistol in my purse."

"A pistol. You?"

"Me," she said, laughing, putting her finger on her chest.

"Why did you do that?"

"When there was shooting, and I had to go places, I would hitch rides with other crazy people and take a pistol with me. If you ride with crazy people, you need a way to defend yourself."

"You don't have a pistol today, do you?"

"No, but I might need one."

I could tell she was kidding. "Is the ambulance driver crazy?"

"Well, he's Lebanese."

We laughed.

"How did you feel with a pistol?"

"Strong and cocky."

After a moment she added, "But I have something else now," reaching into a pocket of the coat. She leaned to hand me a tiny card.

The Arabic words, in her handwriting, said, "The Lord is my shelter."

"You told me I should learn some of those verses," she said, "and I tried, but... I wrote that while I was waiting outside a hospital emergency room. I can't even remember the rest."

"It's enough." I couldn't remember the rest, either, because I knew it best in English and was surprised, seeing that the Arabic word for shelter was the same as the word on signs pointing to bomb shelters.

"It helped," she said.

And I said, "I'm glad," knowing that a gift given had come back to me.

153

She tried to put on her fierce teacher-face and said, "What's the French word for shelter?"

"*Abri.*"

"Bravo. You must have a good French teacher."

I held out the little card, smiling, and she put it into her pocket again.

"Some of the fighting was very close to here," she said. "Were you afraid?"

Was she still testing me? If so, I would flunk, because I had not felt protected by our shelter. I told her the truth. "No, because I was hurting, and then I was sleepy. Well, actually, I was afraid, but not of the gunfire. I thought nobody would come to see me. I was afraid of being alone all day."

The siren sounded briefly, hoarsely, like a signal of horror and loss, almost under my window, and she jumped up. "You underestimated me, didn't you?" She was smiling and looked almost cocky. She loves to surprise people with what she can do.

"I guess so. Did you rescue anyone else today?"

"You mean anyone besides the boy downstairs?"

"No. I mean anyone besides me; I was planning to die if you didn't come."

She was halfway to the door and turned back, her face tense again. She said, "You have to get well. You just have to."

"I know. I have to."

"I'll help. I'll come every day and see that you take care of yourself. Roger and I will order you around and make you do what we say."

"I'm sure of it. I can feel it coming."

She seemed satisfied and turned toward the door again. I was so afraid to let her leave.

I said, "I wish you could stay longer," and she came back and kissed me on both cheeks.

Two minutes later I heard the siren start and keep going, its voice rising to an urgent cry—out to the street, down the hill, getting farther and farther away. The sun was going down, out of sight, into the sea, and the flares it sent up were caught in the windows of mountain towns. I followed the moaning of the siren, praying for the guns to wait, to keep waiting.

A nurse put my flowers out again. I watched her carrying them in front of her, one by one—the tulips, the violets, the mums, the roses, the jonquils, the plant with pointed leaves—thinking, Tony, Nadia, Georgette, Roger, the pastor, Saeed and Allison. And Amineh. She came. That was a whole bouquet of crazy, lovely things. Crazy people were out in the battle, trying to rescue the wounded, visiting the sick.

It came to me, slowly, majestically, like a moonrise over the mountains, that the varieties of love are endless and startling. Maybe everybody knows this, I thought. Surely I have always known this, but all that evening it was new and hung in the room like a banner, like something I could touch and be healed.

I was so tired and didn't care. They gave me drugs, and I stayed awake. The terrifying world was a wonderful place in which shelters opened over our heads like umbrellas, rescue squads appeared, maybe angels stood around, for all I knew.

The Bus to Poplar Bluff

Before we ever boarded the bus, the black man wearing the mother-of-pearl necklace put his arm around the shoulders of the white girl who kept twisting a hank of her hair. The couple who were seeing her off reprimanded him; he claimed, "I didn't touch her"; and the possibilities were already evident.

We passengers were starting to collect stupidly in front of the loading door, the way people do in stations, eager to escape the triteness and irrelevance of the waiting room and get on with real life. The bus was already late.

When a blond dumpling of a girl about eight months and three weeks pregnant, all stuffed into a red knit jumpsuit, joined the group, heads turned, everyone paid attention. One couldn't not notice her. She was as bright and tight and light as one of those doll-shaped balloons at K-Mart.

She dropped her bag and said to the man with the beard and the ponytail, "Will you watch this? While I run over to the snack shop?" And she bounced across the room, exactly as a ball would, her bounces decreasing in depth and increasing in frequency as she neared the kiosk. She came back with both hands full of candy bars, pushed all but one into her bag and then tore the brittle wrapping off the one.

A country woman in white athletic shoes and socks shuffled up to the edge of the group and tried to be invisible. I call her a country woman to be polite. She wore a pink plaid dress, too heavy for the summer weather. Her hair was graying, neglected; her upper lip long and protruding; her anger showed, though she didn't want it to. She would forget that anyone could see her, look vicious, and then, catching my eye, smile a quick, trapped, necessary-to-please kind of smile.

Another woman craved our attention. She made loud remarks to no one in particular, trying to draw someone, anyone, into a conversation. "Last time I did this, we were two hours late; I swore never again and now here I am. Some people never learn." And after no one responded: "My husband will be waiting and mad as hell." One couldn't not hear her, but I was careful not to even glance her way.

The man with the ponytail was not so wise. He said, "Maybe he will call to see if the bus is on time."

She rammed through that little opening somehow with the story of her day—a monologue about the shoplifter she had seen in a department store, how she had witnessed this ridiculous crime, and then the security guard had come. Not that she had called him. No sirree, she minded her own business. That was the best policy.

And the one who twisted her straight hair, who was somehow not competent, who might be a sister of the woman who was standing by to put her on the bus, produced anxiety by her silence. The sister kept telling her again and again, "Johnny will meet you. Don't worry; he'll be there. Don't even think about it on the bus. Just relax and enjoy the ride." Was she listening or not listening? Her face remained blank, and she wound the stub of hair on her finger.

Two nice, healthy-looking boys, college students I supposed, chattered and laughed and chattered and laughed. They carried small backpacks and tennis rackets and looked cool in cut-off jeans. One of them, the smaller one with the lean muscles, wore a yellow T-shirt with a drawing of a mosquito covering the front. There were words above and below the drawing, but I could not see them completely. I liked the boys' smooth faces and clear eyes, but their talk was obscure—very fast and clever, so personal and idiomatic they knew no one would understand, least of all some grandma with her bag full of lollipops and storybooks. Would they determine that much, the way I had already put together their age, their dress, their speech and decided they were students? The boys laughed a lot at each other's remarks, but quietly, keeping it private, polite.

And then the black man, a head taller than anyone else, leaned this way and that, from the top, like a tree caught in a capricious wind. He bumped people, saying, "Excuse me, sir. No offense intended," speaking hoarsely, very slowly and carefully, with slurs and hesitations. When he turned, I saw the necklace shiny-white against his skin, with a white cross dangling at the bottom, in the "V" of his shirt, and because it took my eye, I missed at first the long scar across his neck, a thick pale line just above his Adam's apple.

Once he pushed past everyone, demanding, "Open the damned door," stumbled out to the bus and got on board. A few moments later he was back, weaving drunkenly, asking the group, "What's wrong?" His voice had a damaged, raspy sound. Everyone ignored him. And suddenly he seemed drawn to the woman-child who twisted her hair. He made a place for himself beside her, looked down and said, "You O.K.?" She didn't answer, and then he put his arm around her.

The man who was with the girl said, "Keep your hands to yourself." And his wife said, "Who do you think you are?"

"Joey," he said, putting out his hand. "Pleased to meet you."

"Keep your hands off the girl," the man said.

"I didn't touch her," and he held up both hands to prove it. His hands were very long and elegant, the palms almost white.

"Don't sit by her on the bus. You hear me?"

"I hear ya. I won't do nothin'. No offense, O.K.?"

Through it all, a man in rimless glasses, a man with a burned-orange mustache and an unchallengeable face, kept reading his book, a thick paperback with bent corners. The troubled woman twisted her hair. The fat future mother ate chocolate bars. The talker talked. And I kept thinking...

Oh, yes, there was Jenny. Me. Even at the time I almost forgot that I was a member of this accidental group—not just an observer, but a person on a journey, with others who journeyed. I was interested only in arriving. Whatever happened on the bus, it would be over in three hours, and I would see my small grandson. Jeff would find that I was a stranger. (I am an alien in the place where I live and a stranger in my own family. This is an occupational hazard.) He would turn his face away, and I would have only six days to change that.

Our driver came, in a rumpled uniform, and took tickets at the steps of the bus. He had a face like those little smiley drawings, simple and round and sincere. He apologized. He complimented our patience. He gave women discreet support under one arm saying, "Watch your step, darlin'." He let the protective couple get on with their charge, choose her seat and put her bag in the overhead rack.

Joey boarded last. From my seat several rows back from the door, I noticed that the driver conversed with him. In the quiet of my head I said, "He's drunk. Don't let him get on."

But he got on and walked with his head bent, because the ceiling was so close. He clutched the backs of the seats on either side, bumped one or two but went decisively to the back row. So far so good.

The talker had already sized up the driver as a willing conversationalist, so she sat across the aisle from him on the front row. She was wearing bright shorts and a white blouse with a big flower painted on the front.

I withdrew against a window, leaving my bag in the seat beside me. The bus smelled faintly of fuel exhaust and sweat and stale tobacco. My seat tipped back comfortably; the footrest felt just right under my flat shoes. With a magazine across the knees of my slacks, in case I needed something to make me appear busy, I intended to watch Missouri go by. Not that I am antisocial; I just know that after people say, "Where are you going?" they then say, "Where do you live?" The answer to this question arouses too much interest. It risks a political argument. "What do you do there?" follows and is also a tricky question. The answer can be stated in different ways, and the way should be chosen to suit the questioner and the occasion, or the way I feel at the moment about explaining my motives.

We almost got out of St Louis before trouble started. With broad swings around corners, sighing of air brakes and jolly remarks from the driver, we had reached a long straight highway through the suburbs. Beautiful houses with green lawns floated past the window. Tall trees overhung a peaceful street. Every couple of years I get this treat, a glimpse of my country, moving by, moving on.

The driver and the woman on the front row were talking about the merger of two bus lines. He was telling her that the drivers of one line lost all their longevity.

"That's a cryin' shame," she said.

The fat girl in the red jumpsuit bounced up to the front, like when she went for the candy bars, and plopped down behind the driver. "You know that... that big man, who was dizzy and stuff?"

"Yeah. The black man?"

"Joey. His name's Joey. He's pukin' in the bathroom," she said. "I thought you ought to know."

"Thank ya, darlin'. I 'preciate you tellin' me." And to the talker he added, "He better not be drunk. I asked him if he was drunk, and he told me he was sick. Said he just got outta the hospital."

We were going down a four-lane highway, with a divider strip in the middle, and he suddenly pulled over to the shoulder. "We're still in the city limits," he said. "If he's lyin' to me, I can put 'im off. I don't tolerate drunks on my bus; it ain't fair to the other passengers."

The fat girl went back to her seat, her blue eyes rolling, saying, "He's making me sick." Her skin was as fair as those doll faces, her hair white.

At the bathroom door the driver pounded and called, "Hey, mister. Hey, Joey. Open up." I flipped a few pages in my magazine, past an article about a new reducing diet, and a temptingly illustrated page of cake recipes. And after a moment, I heard him say more quietly, "What's wrong with ya?"

Then I could hear the man's scratchy, whispery reply but not understand, and the driver said, "Why don't you just stretch out there on the back bench? Lotsa room there."

He came back up the aisle again, saying, "Sorry, folks. I am gonna drive you to Poplar Bluff." Behind the wheel, trying to merge back onto the road, he said, "He sure acts drunk, but I don't smell

160

nothin' on 'im. He says he's vomitin' blood. Beats me; I didn't see no blood."

We made it to the freeway and skimmed past thick forests and green fields and birds on telephone wires and an old, tumbled shack, leaning on itself. I imagined my mother, a little girl growing up in such a shack. I thought about my grandma, scrubbing the unpainted floorboards until they were white, hanging mosquito nets over the beds before sundown, lighting the kerosene lamps. The flavor of her cornbread came to me, a flavor impossible to achieve without freshly ground meal and a wood stove. We ate it every evening, with milk warm from the cow, a long time ago when everybody I knew was poor.

On the Missouri landscape a little boy and an old man were walking down a path with fishing poles, and suddenly on the other side of me someone was walking on the seats, throwing a hairy leg over the high back of the one beside me, planting a tennis shoe beside my bag, and then jumping into the aisle. It was one of the boys, who was quickly behind the driver, saying something about "throwing up in the aisle."

The driver turned his head and said, "Which girl, son?"

I knew it was the balloon girl (didn't she warn us?), and then it turned out to be the other one, the disturbed woman who twisted her hair. She was leaning over the arm of the seat into the aisle, and a sour smell was spreading through the bus.

"Jesus!" the talkative woman said and lighted a cigarette.

"We gettin' a plague or somethin'?" the driver said. He called this out, loudly, looking up into his rearview mirror.

And fat Blondie shouted back, "Well, we're all gonna be sick pretty soon."

"The power of suggestion," the boy said, on the way back to his seat. The word above the horrific mosquito was "Missouri" and underneath "State Bird." Our eyes met unexpectedly, and he winked. The message I got was "Neither you nor I will take the suggestion." And then he vaulted over the seat to keep his tennis shoes off the floor.

"We got a rest stop up here in about five miles," the driver announced. "I'll get the bus cleaned up while we're there."

Surprisingly, no one else vomited. While we passengers piled off to buy a drink or stretch our legs, the driver brought on board a pail of water and a mop. He cleaned the aisle, and then the bathroom, chased the sour odor with a nice disinfectant smell, which even neutralized the tobacco smoke. When I got back on and walked down the aisle with my peanuts and fizzy water, the place smelled like the children's room when Rick had been sick and I had cleaned the floor and changed the sheets and washed the rails of his bed.

Behind me the talker said, "Are you the maid on this bus, too?"

"Darlin'..." he said.

"My name's Irene. You can call me Irene."

"Thank you, Irene. I was just gonna say—whatever we need, I'm it. This is the St Louis Mobile Hospital, and I'm the driver, the mechanic, the cop, the nurse, the maid. You name it; I'm it."

Then he turned to the girl who had vomited and said, "You O.K. now, darlin'?"

The girl was twisting her hair. She nodded yes. Her face and her eyes were blank, lacking both concern and character.

Joey got on last again. He had a blurry sort of face, full of knots and knobs and uncertain angles, and his cheeks and chin were covered with a thin, fuzzy beard. I thought this must be the opposite of what they call a "clean-cut" face. He sat down by the girl who was twisting her hair.

"Unh unh," the driver said. "You promised you wouldn't, and I promised the people who put her on."

Joey got up again, but he said, "I'm lonesome back there."

"Come sit up front with me."

"Damn. I don't need no nursemaid and no cop. I just need a friend." His voice then rose to an angry growl. "Is there anybody on this bus who can't sit where he wants, 'cept me?"

"Look, Joey, you remember what happened. You promised you wouldn't sit by the girl. You also promised you wouldn't make me a problem."

So Joey stalked to the back of the bus, his stalk interrupted by a stagger, and flung himself across the seats. And the driver sat down and raised his voice so that most of us could hear. "As I said before, folks, I am gonna drive you to Poplar Bluff."

The sun was low behind the forest. Lines of trees flashed past the orange ball one by one, making the sun blink like moving headlights behind a fence. I turned to see the little town on the other side of the freeway and noticed the woman across from me. Her long protruding upper lip was moving. She was talking to herself, with an angry expression and occasional jerking motions of her head. She sat with her heavy shoes close together, her plaid dress covering the calves of her legs, and clenched her stubby hands into fists. I tried to imagine what she might be upset about—some petty peeve or a deep frustration—tried to visualize the house she lived in, the other people in it, why she was on the bus. Her poverty was apparent. She was a woman, I could see, who would not know how to wear it, if she had a fine dress. And a revelation came to me, by antenna, without basis, that she could not read. Not more than a few road signs, or part of a grocery ad.

This always embarrasses me in the Middle East, to be caught reading Arabic in the presence of Arab women who cannot. But it is I who think this is an outrage and they who find it a marvel.

The woman felt me looking at her, turned her head, and quickly she changed her expression. She smiled, that straight-lipped, trapped, deceitful smile.

I thought I should cross the aisle to her, say something friendly, lay a hand on her closed fist. I don't mean that I reasoned this; it was an impulse, a push from the good spirit behind the universe. And I don't know why I didn't obey. I turned back to the window. A golden field flowed past. Birds flew up from a wire and their curving, fluttering line looked for an instant like the notes of a song against the yellow sky. In the same moment they were gone and I was inexplicably sad, thinking about whole worlds of music I had never heard, the boats I'd missed, the goodbyes that came so soon after hello.

Joey came down then and asked the driver to stop the bus. "I'm

gonna throw up," he said, "and I don' wanta mess up your bus again."
The words had a choked sound.

"Sorry, folks, another unscheduled stop," the driver called out,
but his voice was good-natured, like his face.

Joey stumbled off and leaned over to spit in the small gravel
beside the shoulder of the freeway. I watched deliberately, because I
wanted to know. He gagged, made noises. I saw nothing but white
spittle. When he got back on he said with his scratched voice, " 'Scuse
me, ever'body. See, I got my throat cut and ever since then I been
spittin' up blood." For sure, somebody had cut his throat. The scar
divided his head from his shoulders.

As he went back to his seat, not even looking at the girl, Irene
said behind him, "Jesus!"

"I hope you're prayin', darlin'," the driver said. " 'Cause you're
usin' God's name a lot, and 'cause we could use the prayer."

"That's the truth," she said. "We could use some prayer."

That reminded me to pray, which reminded me of Hikmet,
whose son was kidnapped years ago and never came home. And
Sauson, who goes around all day saying, "If only... If only I... She was
there... I here... She wanted... I said, I'll go... If only I... If only..." ever
since her daughter was killed by a shell. She never changes the subject
or finishes a sentence or hears anything. All I know to do is pray, and
sometimes I forget.

Maybe five minutes passed before I smelled smoke. Not
cigarettes. I smelled burning hair and had turned around in my seat,
when Blondie began shouting, "She set her hair on fire. Her hair is
burning!" The red jumpsuit was bouncing up and down, and she was
waving her hands frantically, as though to ring alarm bells.

Immediately the Missouri State Bird was standing by the girl
who had vomited. "She only singed it a little," he said, in a tone that
meant, "Don't get bent out of shape."

We were stopping again, swinging off the road, everybody
leaning forward, the doors snapping open, our driver jumping out of
his seat like a boy off his bike. He came to her, pushing back his cap
and yanking up his belt, and said, "Darlin', what's the problem?"

"Nothin'," she said, and I was surprised to know she could speak.

"Darlin', why are these other people tellin' me you're settin' your hair on fire?"

She shrugged, twisting her hair.

"Why did you do it, darlin'?"

"It was an accident."

"You set your hair on fire by accident?"

No answer.

From the back Joey said, "Shoulda let me sit there and take care of her."

"Let me have this," the driver said, and took a cigarette lighter from her hand. "I'll just keep it for you 'til we get to Poplar Bluff."

After he put it in his pocket, he lingered beside her and said, "Darlin', you got perty hair, and you are a perty girl. Why you wanta hurt yourself?"

Another shrug. More twisting of her hair.

He trudged back to his seat again and dropped down with a heavy sigh. "This is the St Louis Mobile Asylum, but I ain't no shrink." And he released the air brakes, "Pwhooooosh."

Irene laughed. "You're doing wonderful," she said.

Blondie, in her fire-engine jumpsuit, went up to the seat behind the driver. "I feel safer up here," she said.

"Darlin', you're safe with me, and you're welcome," he said. "Tell us about yourself."

She opened another candy bar and took a big bite. With her mouth full, she told that she was coming down from New York to have her baby in Poplar Bluff.

"Your husband's in New York?" the woman wanted to know.

"Yeah, my boyfriend. He went up and got a job, and then I went. A month after I arrived, I got pregnant. And I wouldn't have my baby in New York for anything. They kill babies up there. When you go in to find out for sure, and they tell you you're pregnant, the next thing they say is, 'Do you want to have it, or do you want to dispose of it?' "

"How come y'all went to New York in the first place?" he asked her.

"I don't know. The grass looks greener farther away."

"Was it greener?"

"Well, no."

"That's the way," he said. "It's never greener, though maybe sometimes a little thicker."

"That's a pretty smart bit of philosophy," Irene said, smoking again, holding the cigarette between red fingernails.

"Well, we were living down south," the girl said, "and my boyfriend is black."

"You gotta be kiddin'," Irene said.

"Darlin'. You don't mind, do you, if I call you darlin'? I call everybody darlin'."

"I don't mind. I think it's sweet."

"Well, darlin', who're ya gonna be with when you have your baby?"

"My sister."

"That's nice you have a sister to look after you."

"Have you given a thought," Irene said, "to what's going to happen in Poplar Bluff when this white-skinned, flaxen-haired young lady produces this little brown baby?"

"Well, I don't care," she said. "My boyfriend is beautiful, and our baby is going to be beautiful."

"Darlin', nobody's doubtin' that," the driver said.

"But Poplar Bluff is Poplar Bluff," Irene added.

"Well, they can't do anything to me."

And the driver said, "That's true, honey. They can't do nothin', except maybe hurt you with their looks and their remarks." He said this with genuine pity.

"When y'all getting married?" the other woman asked her.

"Well, we don't know. We might not get married. We have a good relationship. We're happy, and we don't see a difference, one way or the other."

"See," Irene said, looking toward the driver. "Nobody thinks

166

marriage is sacred anymore."

"This is the nineties," the girl said. "You don't have to marry somebody because you gave him a kiss."

The indignation in her voice was followed by a few moments of silence, and I noticed that the sun had gone down, and the fields were dark and still, with a dome of light above them.

The driver said, "Darlin', so far you've done what you've done because you love that fellow. Now you're gonna do some things because you love that baby."

The tires purred along toward Poplar Bluff, with our driver dimming his lights for approaching cars. I wondered how long it would take to understand the issues in America, to care, to be a part of it all again, or if I ever could.

Irene broke the silence, or maybe they had been talking for a while and I hadn't heard. She said, "Jesus, I don't know how you stand it."

He said, "Today was nothin'. I've had all kindsa things happen. I've had people sneak their little dogs on, and then they start yappin' or get loose, and here I am tryin' to drive the bus with this mutt runnin' around, under people's seats and even here at my feet.

"Once a lady got on with a knife, came up and showed it to me, tol' me she was on her way to kill her husband. I tried to reason with her, but she was too far gone. The worst thing was she said I reminded her of him. That was not fun, drivin' with that woman behind me."

"How do you manage to be so nice to everybody?" the woman said.

"Well, I'll tell you a story," he said.

Wearily, I wished right then to be in Poplar Bluff, hugging Rick and his pretty wife and little Jeff, and I didn't want to hear any more stories, but their voices had pulled me and now I kept listening, even when some words were drowned by the engine.

"Before I was a driver," he said, "I used to do a little carpentry, mostly repairs and the like. And one day I had this job at the home of a very sick lady. I was a real ornery fellow back then, and I tell you,

I could do some mean things and use some bad words. I was up on a ladder, trying to do this job. By the way, I forgot to say that the lady tol' me she didn't have much time to get that fixed, 'cause she was gonna die in a couple of weeks."

"How could she know that?"

"Well, she knew, obviously. So there I was up on the ladder, and the work wasn't turnin' out right, I'd already been obstinate with the lady about how to do the job, and I'm ashamed to tell it, but that was nothin'. I could be real mean. I'd hit my own ma that brought me into the world if she got in my way."

"You don't mean it!"

" 'Fraid I do, but what happened that day was just I banged my finger, and I was mad already, and I let out a stream of words that blistered the paint on the walls. This lady came in and looked up at me. She wasn't any bigger than a ten-year-old, 'cause she'd been shrinking—from old age, ya know, and maybe from this disease she had—and she said, 'Son, it don't cost any more to be nice than it does to be nasty.'

"Now I don't know why, but I started right then to feel a little ashamed. Anyhow, I guess I had to defend myself, so I said, 'Well, it don't pay any better either.' And she said, 'How would you know?'

"That got to me. She hit the nail right on its head, 'cause I hadn't ever tried to be anything but the bullheaded no-good that I was.

"So, I just stood there, lookin' down at 'er and feelin' stupid and corrected. She said, 'Son, I can see there's some real possibilities in you. Now come on down off the ladder and let's talk about it.'

"When I left that day she gave me an extra five-dollar bill. She said, 'Now this is not to spend and it sure ain't a reward for bein' so nasty in my house. This is to keep as a reminder that it don't cost any more to be nice, and that I believe in ya.'

"And I did keep it. I've got it 'til now. Wouldn't spend it if I was starvin'. By the way, she died two weeks later, just like she said she would."

"Oh, my God."

"I thought it was time to straighten up my act, but truthful, I discovered it was hard to be good, even if it don't cost nothin'. So I started tryin' to find out what the good book says, and I found out, all right. I was just a plain ol' son of the devil. Now I promise you I ain't no Mother Teresa yet, but at least I got the right father, and I been trying to make God and her proud of me ever since."

Mrs. Talkative was thoughtful. Finally she said, "That's a story for the *Reader's Digest*. You know those 'unforgettable character' things?"

"Well, I'll never forget her, that's for sure. I owe her a lot, even this job, 'cause people wouldn't put up with me the way I used to be."

"I think you do a good job."

And suddenly Blondie spoke up again. "You are chivalrous," she said, "and chivalry should never die."

I laughed silently, turning toward my reflection in the glass, but he told her, "Thank you for saying that."

All was quiet except for that little island of conversation at the front of the bus, and I looked around in the dimness to see if the other passengers were still there. The two boys were wearing headphones and had their eyes shut. The man with the ponytail was asleep with his mouth open. That girl two rows behind me was still twisting her hair, and I wondered why it hadn't fallen out. The man with the red mustache sat under the little cone of his reading light, turning a page just as I looked, and my angry neighbor across the aisle moved her hands in sharp jerks to emphasize what she was saying under her breath.

Joey came up front once more and asked if anybody had an aspirin. Irene did, but nobody had any water to swallow it with. The driver told him, "Anyway, we'll be there before you can say, Poplar Bluff, Missouri."

We drove in past the fast-food places and the bowling alley and Wal-Mart. While the driver was still parking the bus I saw my tall son with a handsome little boy on his shoulders, and I said to myself, Is that my own grandson?

As soon as he had kissed me, Rick told Jeff to say, "Hi,

Grandma," but the child looked past me and, with a jab of his finger, said, "Big bus!" I liked the way he had already learned not to lose control when he was shy. I liked the force of his 'b's. In fact, I was already so much in love with him that I forgot to notice the other passengers, the directions they went, if they were met, anything. But they came back to my mind later, and I described them all one evening over the dinner table and got a lot of laughs.

Little Jeff accepted my lap as a place to read stories and remembered me for at least a few hours. Rick wrote that all of the day I left he kept saying, "Where's the gramma go?" But, of course, he couldn't understand the answer.

A week later I was back in Beirut doing the things I do (being there is one of the good impulses I have obeyed) and, according to the normal pattern, everything was flying loose: rockets, wild words, dead cease-fires, tempers. Some people were so paranoid they couldn't leave their houses. A couple Roger and I knew wouldn't ride in a car together or sit in the same room, figuring to reduce the possibilities that their children would be orphans. Others thought this was sick behavior and tried to persuade them to take more risks and live a little. I read in a magazine that inmates of the mental hospital were lulled to sleep by the pounding of guns, and we were astonished to discover that thieves roamed the neighborhood while the rest of us were in shelters. It was impossible to know who was crazy.

Trying to make us laugh, I said to Roger, "This must be the bus to Poplar Bluff."

I talked a lot about my trip, especially about the notable bus driver, who, once I was back in Lebanon, had attained great stature in my mind. What a lot of difference he was making in his world. Roger said that maybe I should have enlisted him to come out and help us. He was joking, of course, but I considered the idea seriously for a while. Then I thought, On the other hand, they really need him there in Missouri.

The Chameleon's Wedding Day

SEPTEMBER 1974

Amineh was eleven that summer, spindly and fragile, all eyes and teeth and joints and feelings, and had never taken seriously the possibility that she would be a woman. A doctor maybe. A famous playwright. But not an adult. Irrelevant to any of that, she had noted resentfully certain injustices in the structure of the world. She had to do chores in the house while her brothers were building a raft.

Just as Milad and Dory, still clutching their breakfast sandwiches, practically tumbled out the back door into this adventure, her mother said, "Amineh, you haven't made the beds yet."

"Why do they never make their beds?" she said. It was not even a question, because she knew there would be no answer. There was no way to discuss with her mother the why of anything. "*Haik*," she might say. "It's that way," not even listening, not even looking at her.

Girls were responsible—for food, for cleanliness, for order. Colette, on the other hand, was as old as Amineh and didn't work in the kitchen. She had to take dancing lessons, though she did not want to "stand on her toes and leap like an idiot." It hurt, she said. But her mother made her do it, and the women in the neighborhood had been saying all summer that Colette was beautiful, and she should learn things like dancing.

Amineh went upstairs, and while she was pulling the sheets tight over heavy mattresses and punching long, hard pillows into clean slips, she could hear the boys down by the chicken house. Milad was already pounding nails and Dory was talking in a happy, morning voice, excited. His voice was high and sweet, because he was only six years old. And when he talked to Milad, Amineh could hear it in his voice that he thought Milad was clever and strong and could do anything.

She went to the window and looked out. Milad's head was bent over his work, such earnestness in his posture. His straight hair was uncombed, with twigs of it sticking in crazy directions. They had finished fastening the small logs together the day before. It was Amineh who had found a picture in a book and told him how to do it, and she had run back and forth between the clothesline and the raft to offer advice and lend a hand. Now he was nailing a kind of floor into place over the logs, using some old gray boards left over when their father built the chicken house. Baba had said they could use it. Dory was helping, holding down the board by sitting on it while Milad pounded. "Ow," he was saying, "it hurts my bottom!" But he was laughing and his slender face was shining.

The lovely days of summer were almost gone. In less than two weeks they would pack up everything—their clothes, the eggplant pickles she and her mother had made, the fig jam, the mulberry juice, even some of the cooking utensils and dishes, and they would go back down to their house in the city. She could almost see the house from this window. If she let her eyes start at the sea—so blue today, fuzzy out on the horizon but bright near the coast—she could follow the road, starting at the harbor—lots of ships standing in the harbor today—all the way to the broad flat top of her school. And one of those rusty red roofs on the other side of the street was theirs.

From that house, even sometimes in Broummana on still nights, but especially in that house so near the sea, they could hear the hoarse, lonely horns of the ships. When she was a very little girl Baba had told her that the sound of the horns in the harbor meant it was time for children to go to bed. For years she had hurried into her pajamas if she heard the voice of a ship, eager not for sleep but for their evening story time.

She leaned her elbows on the windowsill and thought about it. She wanted to go, because when school started she would have more books to read and fewer chores to do. But summer was still the best. Summer on the mountain could be the very best part of living, if only she could just be outdoors all day.

Blue-green beetles were flying in the garden, dark streaks under the pine trees, bright above the grapevines, "crack" against a windowpane, "buzz" into the tall grass. It was easy to catch one, and though it squirmed and scratched and tickled her closed hand, she could tie a string to a jerking leg and turn the beautiful and horrible creature into a furious kite. But she had to wash the dishes and sweep the kitchen floor.

When she turned around she saw her pajamas lying by the bed, swooped them up and threw them onto the closet shelf. Before she shut the door she looked at herself in the long mirror on the back of the door. Am I a pretty girl, she wondered. No one had said so. She looked at her long arms and legs, sticking out of pink shorts and a T-shirt. She could not say what was right or wrong about them. Her eyes were... She focused on her eyes, which stared back at her darkly. They looked, well... surprised, curious. It was because they were big and because her eyebrows went up in a high curve. Her hair was thick and curly, too thick to brush and looked the same whether she did or she didn't.

She was very brown. Grandmother didn't like that. Grandmother always told her to stay out of the sun or she would be black as an African. That was a silly exaggeration and once Amineh had told her so, but her mother had said, "Shame, Amineh! Don't speak to Taita like that."

Amineh stood up on her bare toes, lost her balance and tried again. Colette was right. Why should pretty girls be tortured, learning to dance on their toes? And wouldn't it make a girl's feet callused and hard, like the feet of the porter who ran around the souk, barefoot, with a basket strapped to his back? For ten piastres this man would carry a basketful of vegetables to their home, when she and Baba went shopping. All the way Amineh bumped into people (and her daddy told her to apologize) because she couldn't take her eyes off the porter's feet, which were swift and dirty and hard like an animal's hooves. Taita said that Amineh's feet would be like that if she didn't wear her shoes.

Milad must have smashed his thumb. Hearing him howl, she slammed the closet door and ran down to finish her work in the kitchen. Milad came in, his face flushed and contorted, holding up his left thumb for everyone to see. Amineh said, "Don't worry. I'll come and do the nailing. Five minutes, I need. Just five minutes," and she was running hot water into the plastic pan in the sink.

In the afternoon they finished the raft. Milad nailed the final boards in place, determined to be the one, clenching his teeth and holding his damaged thumb in the air. Amineh searched for just the right pole to push them across the pond. (They had debated about a sail and decided that a pole was more appropriate.) While they worked, a yellow cat stalked a grasshopper through the brown, dusty weeds, then lost interest and sidled up to rub her leg. She said, "Kitty can go with us, if she wants."

"Unreasonable," Milad said. "Whoever heard of a cat on a raft?"

"We will see," she said.

The cat belonged to a neighbor who also had a sadistic kid named Charbel, but Amineh understood that cats do not belong to people. Their independence made people dislike them, so she had appointed herself defender of cats, and she protected them from cruel boys who pulled their tails (though she was afraid to say anything to cranky women who kicked them). This duty required diligence, because there were even more bad boys than cats in Broummana. Boys named Charbel were especially wicked. She didn't know why, but anyone named Charbel was likely to be a little devil.

The hour of the great voyage had arrived. The raft, sitting in the dead weeds just outside the chicken yard, looked lost and useless, like something that had fallen to earth out of a dream. But in the water it would be splendid. They had cautioned one another not to breathe a word to any adults or even drop a clue. ("Act bored," Amineh said.) While their mother was resting she went to the kitchen and, working nimbly and quietly (experience was a valuable thing, she decided), made sandwiches for their trip. Then she called Colette on the phone and whispered loudly, "Hurry, we're ready."

When he saw Colette, Milad said, "No girls allowed!" He pulled up his lower lip and tried to look tough when he said it. Dory, loyal Dory, thought he should take Milad's side and echoed him, "No girls allowed." Then he laughed his high, sweet laugh and said, "But Amineh is a girl."

And Milad, flustered, said, "Amineh doesn't count. Anyway, it's a small raft. Three people are enough."

At the moment Amineh really did not know whether it was a compliment or an insult that she did not count as a girl, but she decided to think about that later. She said, "If Colette doesn't go, I will tell Baba you threw an egg at me." (She had been effectively holding this over his head for three weeks.)

No sooner was this settled than Charbel showed up and assumed himself invited, and Amineh could not object. Besides, they really needed his help to carry their clumsy, wonderful vessel. Amineh gave Dory the lunch sack and the pole. She and Milad and Colette and Charbel carried the raft and were surprised, all of them, by how heavy it was. The boards of its deck were various lengths and rough on the end. Amineh got a splinter in her finger but didn't care. They struggled quietly down the path, stumbling past Taita's house, with Dory giggling and Kitty at his heels.

Amineh said, "Look, Kitty wants to go with us."

Milad said, "What have you got in the sack? Tuna fish?"

It was tuna fish. And Amineh could hear Baba saying, "A cat will sell an olive orchard for a kilo of fish." She didn't like that saying, because it made cats sound stupid.

Milad was acting big again. He was saying, "When we get there everybody has to do as I say. I'm the captain of the ship."

The sun was high in the sky and hot. Dandelions as big as tennis balls fell apart as the children brushed past them, and there was a smell of weeds and dust. A small gray cloud floated over Beirut, its shadow moving with it toward the mountain.

The path down the hill plunged precariously in spots, offered rough stone steps in others, curved around a gnarled olive tree and cut through a patch of onions and lettuce. When they passed the springhouse they could hear a frog croaking and just below was the wide terrace and the pond.

Really it was an irrigation pool, fed by the small spring, and a hole in the bottom of it could be shut to collect more water or opened to let the water run down through a system of little canals to the gardens and fruit trees. Even in late summer the pool was full, and water was flowing down into a channel that angled off toward old man Khalil's cabbage patch. In one corner of the pool, a big frog sat on a clump of green slime and stared.

Amineh and Milad rested their raft on the edge of the pool, while they took off their shoes. (Amineh had decided to wear her shoes while walking outdoors, just in case.) Then they stood up and gave the raft a few tugs and pushes, and it splashed into the water. Dory jumped and squealed, "It floats! It floats!"

"Hand me that," Amineh said, taking the pole from him before he could whack someone accidentally. And Milad said, "Of course it floats." Then he and Charbel jumped into the water and held the side of the raft against the edge of the pool while Dory and Colette went aboard, Dory jumping, Colette putting one foot cautiously, then the other. (Soft and white, Amineh noticed.) Amineh stepped on, carrying Kitty in the crook of one arm and the pole in the other.

"Sit down," Milad ordered, and they all sat down. The floating cloud blotted the sun momentarily.

Charbel climbed aboard, rocking the boat and flinging water everywhere. The cat squirmed in her arms, but Amineh held on tight while rubbing Kitty's head and speaking softly, "Don't be afraid, Kitty, you're with me and everything is fine."

"It's a good opportunity to drown that cat," Charbel said, and Amineh dared him with a sharp look.

Milad threw up one wet leg and sort of rolled onto the deck. The raft wobbled and then righted itself immediately. He stood up, took the pole from the bend of Amineh's arm and put one end into the water. When he pushed, an expanse of water, already too big to step across, stretched out between them and the shore and mirrored a wobbly image of the cloud outlined by sunshine. Dory said, "We're moving. *Yalla*, let's go." He had two bright-pink spots on his fair cheeks.

Milad pushed with the pole again, and the trees and the terrace wall shifted sideways. Amineh thought, "We could take this to the sea and ride on the waves."

A few dusty raindrops fell on their hot skin. Colette said, "It's raining and the sun is shining."

What happened then happened very slowly, though too quickly for anyone to move or to speak. This was maybe the first time Amineh ever noticed that something could happen suddenly, be over before one knew it was going to happen, but at the same time get slowed down somehow and just hang in the air like something that went on happening for a long time.

Amineh thought, "It's raining before time. It shouldn't rain in summer." But she didn't speak, because Kitty, who was the first to know what would happen, tore out of her arms and leaped from the raft to the shore, barely making it, her rear legs dangling and scratching on the concrete ledge, just as Amineh felt water on the seat of her shorts and saw the floorboards already wet and going under. She looked up and saw the children's faces full of astonishment and disbelief and belief and fear, as the water rose around their seats and then their waists, and the ends of Colette's hair. For a moment their knees were still out of the water, and they had all lifted their hands, the lunch sack still in Dory's.

In total silence they went down. It was already over when she heard Colette say, "We're sinking! We're sinking!" and heard Dory scream and saw the lunch sack flying and Dory's arms flailing and realized that she was in water to her shoulders, still sitting on the raft which was sitting on the bottom of the pond. Milad, not having made a sound, was standing in water above his knees, still holding the pole in position against the bottom of the pool.

Too late she felt terrified and jumped to her feet, getting water and a foul green taste in her mouth, at the same moment that Milad let the pole fall and leaped after Dory who was coming up gasping. Colette was standing in the water, trembling, her clothes wet and muddy and her beautiful brown hair dripping, and when Amineh walked toward her she discovered that the bottom of the pool was gooey with mud and cluttered with slimy sticks and stones and wiggly things. She made a face and a throw-up noise, and Colette said, "What is my mother going to say?"

Charbel yelled, a yell of utter joy, because disaster was his favorite situation, a condition to which he could contribute. And he began smashing the water with his hands, throwing waves of it on the one who hated disaster the most—Colette.

Khalil came running then, shouting of course. Khalil always acted like he was leading a riot. He screamed a lot of bad words. He said that they knew it was not allowed to swim in the pool.

Milad, climbing out of the water, said, "We're not swimming."

Khalil said, "Shut up. Don't tell me you are not swimming when I can see you are swimming." His face was red and ugly.

Just at the right time their father appeared. He was wearing his colonel's uniform and looked very big and important. He strolled down the path as though he were just inspecting his neighbor's lettuce. Khalil stopped shouting and Charbel stopped splashing.

"What's going on down here? Civil war?" Baba was using his teasing voice, and Khalil seemed embarrassed for a moment, but then he started yelling again.

Baba turned to Milad and said, "What happened, son?"

"My raft sank."

"You put your raft in the irrigation pond?"

"Yes, sir."

"Where were you going? To America?"

"No, sir."

And then Baba said to Khalil, "Milad is a very clever boy. Always building or inventing something."

He walked with Khalil along the edge of the pool and together they discovered that the flow of water to the canals was a mere drip.

178

This led to more shouting and to Khalil's accusation that the raft was plugging the hole where the water went down. The children just stood there, cool and dripping and watching the men, except Milad who was staring at the water, a tragic captain whose ship had gone down.

Finally, Milad went back into the water and with many suggestions and instructions from the bank, he found a wine bottle, a bicycle tire, a tin can, and the raft, which already seemed to Amineh like a summer dream, a funny and wonderful dream that did but didn't quite happen. Though Milad couldn't say whether or not it was covering the hole, it seemed to be sucked down by some force, perhaps its own dark fate. He tried to pick it up, slipped and tumbled backward, coming up again with mud and green slime on his skin and his clothes.

Khalil started shouting again; someone was going to get very messy doing this job, and it wouldn't be him. But Baba said, "I will take care of it tomorrow." More shouts, to which Baba responded, "If it overflows, the grass will get watered and then your cabbages," and he began leading the children up the path toward home.

Amineh noticed then how a path back home was so different from the path going away. Ascending the hill, they saw how the terraces along the way were supported by walls of yellow rocks, with dead grass hanging out between the stones, and they saw the underside of leaves they had seen from the top before. She wondered where Bisi had gone to lick her back legs dry and she thought, "Summer is over."

Dory, who had the mess from the bottom of the pool on his hands and the seat of his pants, as well as a few smudges on his pretty face, took his father's hand and said, with awe in his voice, "I drowned."

Again it rained a few big, splashy drops and Amineh expected Colette to say, "It's raining, and the sun is shining," but Colette was worried about being dirty and wet, so Amineh said it herself.

Baba looked up at the sky, and said, "Yes, the chameleon is getting married. Let's watch for a rainbow."

Dory said, "Our lunch drowned."

Taita's big rooster, beautiful and mean, was fighting with a young, small cock, creating a storm of shrill squawks, bright feathers and flying dust.

Milad, close to tears, kicked the gatepost and said, "It sank! Why did it sink?"

Charbel pulled back his arm and flung a stone. He was lucky, and it went through the wire fence and scattered the chickens.

SPRING 1991

Sun and shadows were chasing one another across the scarred, still lovely, face of Lebanon, playing against the broken wall of a battered house and running through fields that were bursting with new life. The whole mountainside looked as though a giant pot of green paint had been poured out to dribble over the edges of the terrace walls and into the cracks in the sidewalks, and here and there, along the street, between the stone houses, almond trees were dropping white blossoms among the clover.

A young woman stepped down from a yellow bus, looking a lot like a little girl, with her long hair and her school satchel. She was a high-school literature teacher, though the eleven-year-old she used to be was barely lost in her slight body and asserted herself still in the tilt of the young woman's chin. Waving at the departing bus, she turned and started down the stone stairs toward her house, noticing that Beirut looked damp and bedraggled, half-clothed in tattered scraps of clouds.

How she had loved this place on the mountain, when she was a child, loved looking down on the city from the cool green heights, seeing the curves of the land, firm and dark, against a mercurial sea. Sometimes everything that had happened since then felt like only an interruption of real life, and this perception caused moments of genuine confusion about her age. I am twelve, she would think. I must be twelve now, or maybe a teenager. When was I ever twelve? Or sixteen? And sometimes she thought she must be very, very old, because her head was so full of holes. Things leaked out through the holes, so that she did not know anything that happened last October and experienced odd, vacant moments when she could not remember growing up. She worried about this often, thinking that maybe she had been damaged by all the trauma, that she was not normal anymore. Sometimes. But other times she danced and laughed and made cakes for no reason but that she was tired of being sad. She made sudden decisions to be happy and was happy. She said to Dory once, "I belong to God, so if I'm cracked anyplace, it's God's problem."

And he had answered, "Good, if I can't stand you anymore, I'll bring it up with God."

Stopping near the front door, she squatted down to stroke the head of a yellow cat. "Did you miss me, Tiger? Are you as hungry as I am?" Tiger had a torn ear and a bald patch on one leg; he would not let anyone but Amineh touch him.

To enter the house she had to go around a stack of big metal barrels filled with sand, a barricade erected to protect the door from shrapnel. She wondered if maybe they could afford to dismantle it now and how they would manage to move it when they felt really safe; then she pushed on the heavy iron and glass door and called out, "I'm here."

Milad was hunched over his drawing table, under a window in the dining room, and merely grunted a greeting. In this high-ceilinged room with its big table and dark carpet, the light as well as the heat seemed to hang up near the ceiling. Noticing the cold and the dimness, she flipped the switch on the wall. There was no electricity.

She said to the back of his head, "How's Mother?"

And he said, "I don't know. Ask her." And she guessed that it had not been a good day for Milad.

On the dining-room buffet, among the old photographs and the telephone, the plate of keys and coins, and Dory's sunglasses, she found a large brown envelope, addressed to her—familiar handwriting, a return address in Paris. Colette! From Colette in

Paris! She began to tear the flap, almost destroying the envelope, scratching her finger on the metal fastener.

Just then the telephone rang and when she said, "Hello," she heard excitement in her own voice. It was Aunt Samira, who said, "Amineh, tell my sister I am coming for a little visit in half an hour." So Amineh, with a twinge of frustration, thought to save her mail. She would sit down with her letter and a cup of herb tea, and make it an occasion, like old times—Colette and Amineh talking girl talk at the kitchen table.

She found her mother in bed with the curtains drawn and a wet cloth on her head. The room looked tired and cluttered, with stacks of clean laundry on the dresser and the other bed, Baba's bed. The shrapnel holes in the curtains, the crack in the mirror and her mother's uncombed hair were all part of the disarray, the irritation that lived in this room.

"Feeling bad?" she said.

And her mother made an impatient gesture with her hand.

"Aunt Samira called. She's coming to see you."

Her mother turned her face away and sighed. Amineh knew her thoughts—Samira would sit like a queen instead of a sister, expecting to be entertained. Amineh wanted just to leave the dark room and go and make a hot drink, but she sat down, clutching the brown envelope on her lap and said, "I'll make some coffee for the two of you. What shall I do about dinner?"

"I made *kibbeh*, but I didn't bake it yet. Just make a salad." Her mother's voice was listless and disinterested, and Amineh felt imposed upon and angry and, as always if she were angry at her mother, guilty besides. She stayed a while and made small talk, as an act of apology.

On the way to the kitchen, she said to Milad, "What happened today? Did something upset Mother?"

He dropped his pencil on the table, put both hands on the wheels of his chair and swung it around. He had puffy circles under his eyes and looked so much older than twenty-six. He said, "She heard me telling Dory that he should leave."

"I see."

"It's not fair, Amineh. Dory could do anything in the world. He deserves a chance. What does she want? For all her children to sit here and rot?"

"Is that what she heard you say?"

"Not exactly." He turned the chair again and picked up the pencil. Ever since they had been occupied again by foreign troops Milad had been bitterly concerned about Dory.

She looked at his back for a while, trying to guess the rest. She got up and peeped over his shoulder at his drawing and said, "Looks great." One couldn't be tender with Milad; he would mistake it for pity. Neither did she dare to say that he had found himself because of that bullet in his spine, but she felt he was born to be an architect.

Milad moved his ruler and went on working. And she thought to herself that no one had suggested that Amineh go and make something out of her life. They never would. She was a teacher already. Other than that she was only expected to get married and live in the village near her mother. But she would not; she was sure she would not; she hoped she would not.

"Where is Dory?" she said.

He shrugged.

He doesn't have the courage, she thought. Dory would rather "rot" than feel he deserted his brother, or hurt his mother. Lately she had begun to pray a lot for her family—before getting out of bed, before sleeping, and in small desperate moments during the day; waiting at roadblocks, in the classroom, in the middle of conversations, she would say silently, "Here we are, God, in all of these traps inside of traps."

But at that moment, the envelope was burning her fingers, and still standing there behind Milad, she pulled out the paper, a surprising number of sheets. The letter was hardly more than a note. It said, "Happy Birthday, Amineh! Sorry this is late. I really tried to get it to you on time. Remind me of some more good stuff, and I will try to 'keep it for us.' " There behind the scribbled note was a typed story. Amineh read only the title page, then clutched it to her chest and whirled around in a circle. A story by Colette, dedicated to Amineh!

She had kept her promise, the promise made, up by the gate at the top of the stairs, on the day she left. She left for good, *"ah tool"* as people say, an expression that makes one think of the years stretched out like an empty road. For months they had debated it together. Who in their generation had not debated it? Colette had proposed they go together, but Amineh knew that a word about it would put her mother to bed and plunge the household into gloom. None of them knew how acutely she had wanted to go. Like Dory, she kept her longings to herself.

Even conversations about it between her and Colette had been heavy with things neither wanted to say. Colette had been engaged once to a man who went to America (to make a place for her), where he fell in love with an American girl (to keep from being deported, Amineh suspected) and wrote her that he was married. Most of Amineh's college friends had traveled to one country or another; most of them wrote two or three letters and then disappeared. Leaders of lost causes and hunted people left. Assassins escaped. Wealthy politicians traveled, pulled the strings from afar and didn't have to live with the consequences. Amineh sorted it out objectively: they had all been betrayed so many times, but that didn't make it wrong to get off a sinking ship or a crime against the people caught in their cabins below. Colette was a writer with real promise, and her best language was French; she should go. As for herself, it was only frivolous things she wanted to study there in France—art and music and French cooking and photography, whatever looked interesting in the university catalog, things she would probably never use except for pleasure.

When the time came, Amineh had told Colette just to leave without coming to say goodbye, because she lacked the courage to enunciate yet another loss. But at the last moment, nearly, she had lost her nerve; she had run up the stairs and stood in the gate and watched for the car that would be taking Colette to the airport. While waiting, she had imagined herself standing there some other day, the terraces going down the hill like steps, as always, their summer brown giving way to winter green, fog rolling in from the sea. Across the road, Selim's benzene station would be blackened by fire but pumping gas again. It would rain into the shell of their house in Beirut. (Only a few days ago she had discovered that it still stood there; she had gone to see and found it forsaken and hollow like a brainless skull.) The rain would fall on Baba's grave, and her mother would get a headache. Everything would go on the same. At school she would try to read Gibran with kids who wouldn't understand, because they couldn't remember peace and never really knew what it meant to have a country. Milad crippled, Dory in a bind, her mother withdrawing, and Colette gone, a new dimension to her loneliness.

She had stood there, in the cool of November, seeing these pictures of her life, seeing that her story had been vandalized, torn into fragments, stuck together wrong, and patched with pieces that didn't belong. The result was completely false, like a bad dream or an accident. History had been derailed, leaving her standing by the road, afraid and embarrassed. But Colette will climb out of the wreckage, she thought, and tell them who we really are. And when she had thought some more she added: And make us remember; that's the main thing.

A car passed, stopped, backed up. A door opened. A red high-heeled shoe and a shapely leg emerged, and there was Colette, her brown hair shining, an unusual softness in her dark eyes, the lashes a little damp. Struck by her beauty, Amineh had thought, She'll have Paris at her feet.

"How can I just go," Colette said, "and you standing here in the gate?"

Without preamble, Amineh had said, "Don't forget the good things. When you write, I mean."

"The good things." Colette had repeated her words with deliberate flatness, considering their meaning. "For instance?"

And Amineh had tried to think what she meant. "Well, the jokes we make up about ourselves... going to church and singing even under the shells... the fun we had when we were kids. Remember our raft?"

It had just popped into her head after all those years.

"What... yeeee, the raft!" Colette had put both manicured hands to her astonished face, and they had begun laughing, Colette tilting back and forth in her high heels. "We were a mess, and our poor mothers so wanted us to be ladies."

"You were supposed to be a ballet dancer."

"Imagine."

"Wasn't it fun?"

"It was wonderful."

"Write those happy things. O.K.? Keep them for us."

And Colette, with that little toss of her head that always meant she had decided, said, "I will. I will write a story just for you. As soon as I unpack my typewriter." She kissed her quickly and started backing away as she spoke and paused in the open car door to wave and say, "I'll put it in your birthday card." She had sounded happy and sure.

The car had been already moving when the door shut, the red high heel going in last. And Amineh had stood there alone for a while, already pricked by doubt and remembering that she had vowed once to forget anyone who left.

Amineh stopped whirling around long enough to read the first sentence of the story. There she was—eleven years old, a scrawny little scrap of a person, already restless. She smiled and walked, while reading, into the kitchen, filled a tiny coffeepot and put it on a burner, opened the cold oven and put in the *kibbeh* without looking at it. She read while stirring the coffee into the water. There was Milad—still brave and innocent, nailing scrap lumber together, with Dory sitting on the edge of a board, squealing.

Without knowing she did it, she heard a knock on the door, let Aunt Samira in, served coffee in her mother's room and ran back to the kitchen. She sat on the edge of a chair then and read to the end. It was all there, the beetles, the cat who never had any name but Kitty, the dandelions disintegrating, the tensions and loyalties, the swift, slow, sad and funny sinking of their raft. Khalil was in it. Amazing, it seemed at this moment, that Khalil had kept his sanity, with all rules broken and no one listening when he yelled. And odd that they thought he was old then, and seventeen years later he was still just old. (A mortar had fallen in the middle of the irrigation pond one day, blowing the water away and flooding the gardens suddenly, in all directions. Amineh always wished she could have seen that explosion of water. Just thinking of it made her laugh.) Baba was there in the story, more real than he had been for years, assuring Dory that he had not drowned.

Charbel was in it, poor, mean Charbel, who had disappeared without a trace, on the same day that a car bomb mangled fifty people. His parents thought he was one of the victims, though his body was never found. Some people thought he was the driver of the car, and that the person with the remote control had detonated the bomb too soon.

It was Dory's walking into the kitchen that made her realize she had forgotten about Aunt Samira (had she gone already?) and forgotten to drink tea, and (oh no!) she had not lighted the oven before she put in the *kibbeh*. She would have to take it out and start over with a hot oven. She apologized that dinner would be late.

Dory said, "The electricity came," and turned on the light. Then he stood there, leaning against the sink, unconcerned about dinner, his brown eyes thoughtful. The shadow of a heavy beard made the lower half of his face dark. Black curls were falling down on his forehead; if he noticed, he would think he needed a haircut. She remembered his soprano voice, his high, sweet laugh when he was helping Milad build the raft. Suddenly she could see Baba and Dory walking hand in hand up the path toward home that memorable afternoon, and, as though it had happened on the same day, she recalled that the last thing Baba did before his death was to sell his last piece of land to pay for Dory to go to college. But Baba was a patriot, and he believed in Lebanon. To keep one's money in dollars or francs undermined the Lebanese lira, he said. And so most of Dory's college money was lost when the lira collapsed, and now he had no degree and no job.

Supposing he really could "do anything," what kind of chance did her little brother want? Could they find a way?

"Dory," she said, "what did Milad say to you today? The thing that upset Mother."

"Well," he said, "it was just silly. He said, 'Don't think about the rest of us. Get out of here while you can still walk.' "

"Why is that silly?"

He moved the muscles of his face in a way that said, "Why should I state the obvious?"

And she said, "It's not so silly. In a way, you're already crippled, too. Because you can't decide what you want. Or because you're afraid to tell us."

"I have to wait and see," he said. "If Lebanon walks, I can walk."

"If, if, if," she said sharply. "Dory, we have been waiting since we were children for Lebanon to walk. And it's backwards. What is Lebanon? It's you and I. We're Lebanon."

He said nothing, and she picked up the story, tapped the bottom edge of the pieces of paper against the table, and slid them back into the torn envelope. Colette would be a successful writer, even a famous writer. She was sure of it. Someday everyone would read about their raft. Meanwhile, it was her own story, her birthday present. She would read it in bed tonight and laugh and cry. And she would write to Colette and remind her of some other things: for instance, the day Milad and Charbel stole the nuns' keys and locked everybody into the school. She would give Colette permission to write secrets: it was Amineh who opened the rabbit hutch and let all those wonderful animals go free just before they were scheduled to be skinned and eaten. She would talk about how outrageously happy she was once in a bomb shelter when she finished a debate with herself by deciding that she believed in eternal life. If she started thinking about it, there would be jillions of things.

Dory interrupted her thoughts. He said, "What are you smiling about, sister? Tell me something."

And she said, "I was thinking about some of the fun we've had in our lives, the happy times." And as soon as she said it she thought of sun and shadows sliding across the green terraces and rain falling in the sunshine. It's always like that, she thought—fear that stops our blood from running, followed by the joy of being alive, strong words of God ("I will never leave you nor forsake you") breaking into our pain, love found and love lost. We laughed after our raft sank. We still laugh.

"*Haik al-hayat,*" she said aloud. "*C'est la vie.* That's life." She got up and turned her back to wipe a ridiculous tear.

Dory said, "Are you O.K.?"

When she spoke again, her voice had the commanding tone that she sometimes used in the classroom. "I'm giving you until after dinner to tell me what you'd like to do, and then we'll make a plan, a compromise, a way for me to help you and you to help me. Quick! Set the table, while I make the salad. Put on the white tablecloth and pick some flowers."

From the other room, he yelled, "What are we celebrating?"

And she answered, "Tell Mother dinner is served in ten minutes."

"But Mother has a headache."

"Tell her she has ten minutes to get well."

He appeared at the kitchen door again. "Tell her what?"

Amineh leaned inside the big refrigerator and said, "Tell her Amineh has invented a salad too good to miss. Tell her anything. Tell her the chameleon is getting married, and there's a magnificent rainbow."

When she stood up again, he was staring out at the gathering darkness, looking so puzzled that she laughed.

He said, "I think I'll tell her Amineh has a fever and she had better come and see about it."